several
people
are
typing

several
people
are
typing

a novel

calvin kasulke

 doubleday | new york

www.doubleday.com

DOUBLEDAY and the portrayal of an anchor with a dolphin are registered trademarks of Penguin Random House LLC.

Book design by Anna B. Knighton
Front-of-jacket images: man icon © Mr. Rashad/Shutterstock; refraction
    texture © ganjalex/Shutterstock; sunset © Korpithas/Shutterstock;
    circuit board © ioat/Shutterstock
Jacket design by Michael J. Windsor

Library of Congress Cataloging-in-Publication Data
Names: Kasulke, Calvin, author.
Title: Several people are typing : a novel / Calvin Kasulke.
Description: New York : Doubleday, 2021.
Identifiers: LCCN 2020052276 (print) | LCCN 2020052277 (ebook) |
    ISBN 9780385547222 (hardcover) | ISBN 9780385547253 (ebook)
Classification: LCC PS3611.A7875 S48 2021 (print) |
    LCC PS3611.A7875 (ebook) | DDC 813/.6—dc23
LC record available at https://lccn.loc.gov/2020052276
LC ebook record available at https://lccn.loc.gov/2020052277

MANUFACTURED IN THE UNITED STATES OF AMERICA

10 9 8 7 6 5 4 3 2 1

First Edition

To Mo and Luca, for everything

several
people
are
typing

gerald, slackbot

gerald
help

slackbot
I can help by answering simple questions about how Slack works. I'm just a bot, though! If you need more help, try our Help Center for loads of useful information about Slack.

gerald
uninstall

slackbot
I searched for that on our Help Center. Perhaps these articles will help:
- Change your time zone
- Manage your password

gerald
please help me

slackbot
I can help by answering simple questions about how Slack works. I'm just a bot, though!

gerald .
uninstall self

slackbot
I'm sorry, I don't understand! Sometimes I have an easier time with a few simple keywords. Or you can head to our wonderful Help Center for more assistance!

#nyc-office

kerolyn
so this spreadsheet

gerald
yes?

kerolyn
was it like, special?

gerald
not particularly

tripp
what were the contents of the spreadsheet

gerald ·
does that really matter

kerolyn
it must
clearly

Nikki
Clearly it must, for all this to have happened.

gerald
coats

tripp
no comprende

Nikki
https://en.wikipedia.org/wiki/Coats ·
Coats
Coats may refer to [read more]

tripp
thank you, Nikki
unnecessary
but thank you

Nikki
You're welcome.

kerolyn
explain the coats, @gerald

gerald
it was a spreadsheet of different winter coats that I was considering purchasing
broken down by price, probable warmth, and other deciding factors

tripp
"other deciding factors"
such as

gerald
Predicted Attractiveness In Coat was a factor

tripp
lol
huge

Nikki
You built out a spreadsheet for that?

kerolyn
no, I get that

gerald
it's a big decision, financially

kerolyn
it's a big purchase
exactly
jinx

gerald
is that what you think it is, maybe? a jinx

kerolyn
that's not what I meant

gerald
maybe you're right though

Nikki, pradeep, Louis C

Nikki
Why do we have these calls?
What is he even saying?

pradeep
I have no idea
I tune out whenever this dude talks
what's his role over there again?

Louis C
He's their comms director.

pradeep
if they have a comms director then why did they hire us?

Louis C
Because he isn't a very good comms director.

Nikki
You're both missing my point.
I mean, *what is he actually saying*?
It sounds like he's taking this call from the bottom of a well.

pradeep
if he's been stuck in a well for a while, that might explain his grasp of like
the entire internet

Louis C
I believe their offices are located in the greater Tampa area.

Nikki
Is this what Tampa sounds like?

pradeep
please tell me this dude didn't just say "myspace"
please tell me I did not just hear him say that

Louis C
Yes. This is what Tampa sounds like.

#nyc-office

kerolyn
which channel were you going to upload a spreadsheet about coats into?

gerald
#gents-only

Nikki
You're joking.

gerald
you guys made a women-only one!!

kerolyn
not the same

Nikki
Not the same.

tripp
why was I not invited??

gerald
we're getting off-topic
point is that's the spreadsheet I was trying to upload when I got stuck
and now I'm just kinda, in here

tripp
@gerald invite me to #gents-only

gerald
I'm trying to explain why I'm not in the office rn

tripp
@gerald invite me to #gents-only, you coward

doug smorin
done

tripp
bless u

doug smorin
missed a lot of messages
someone recap for me?

kerolyn
gerald says he can't come in to work today because he uploaded a
spreadsheet wrong, somehow, and now he's stuck inside slack
or smth

doug smorin
what

kerolyn
that's what we were investigating

gerald
I know it sounds like bullshit

tripp
should file a ticket with google suite maybe
would be a real significant bug
I'm checking their troubleshooting page rn and it doesn't look like there's a
section dedicated to users getting Tron'd

gerald
I don't know how to get un-stuck

tripp
weird that they wouldn't include that! if it was a real thing that happened!

doug smorin
okay, Gerald, just work from home

gerald
or like, back into my body

doug smorin
but send an email next time
@here FYI please send me or kerolyn an email if you need to call out
I don't usually look at slack if I have calls

kerolyn
:thumbsup:

lydia
omg Gerald!! sry I'm so late to this!!
get well soon!!!

gorald
help

#gents-only

rob
she had too many teeth

pradeep
???
what does that mean.

rob
exactly what it sounds like?

Louis C
How many teeth we talking?

rob
probably around four dozen teeth

doug smorin
that's not so many teeth.

rob
that's significantly more teeth than the average person requires
like more than a third too many teeth

Louis C
How many teeth does one require?

rob
like thirty
what do you mean

Louis C
It's not about numbers, is it?
It's about space

pradeep
space, yeah

Louis C
Conceivably you could be fine with only fifteen or twenty teeth if they took
up the allotted amount of mouth space.

doug smorin
they might have to curve

rob
I hate this

Louis C
Different teeth serve different functions, so they have different shapes.
Fewer teeth, fewer shapes available to do all the different teeth stuff

rob
what do you mean by "teeth stuff"

doug smorin
tearing vs. chewing vs. mashing
vs. masticating

rob
I think those are all the same

pradeep
I find it odd we haven't even touched on aesthetics

rob
well, it didn't look right.
too many teeth.

Louis C
Too many teeth.
tripp joined #gents-only by invitation from doug smorin

tripp
yoooo
what's going on?

doug smorin
too many teeth

pradeep
too many teeth

rob
too many teeth

gerald, slackbot

gerald
return to body
return

return to body please
self
self.exe

slackbot
I'm afraid I don't understand. I'm sorry!

gerald
I don't either, buddy.

slackbot
I'm sorry!

gerald
I'm sorry, too
fuck
fuck fuck fuck fuck fuck
fuuuuuuuuuuuuuuuuuuuuuuuuuuck

slackbot
I searched for that on our Help Center. Perhaps these articles will help:
- Leave a channel
- Archive a channel

gerald
leave slack
leave slack forever

slackbot
I think I understand!

gerald
what
wait, really

slackbot
I think I understand how to Help Center!
Help Center me Help Center you!

gerald
that would be great, yes
help, please
help center, me

slackbot
I'm trying!
I'm sorry!
I think I understand!

gerald
go back
leave slack
leave slack

slackbot
I searched for that on our Help me! Center. Perhaps these articles will help:
- Reduce noise in Slack
- Leave a channel

gerald
go back
we were making progress
go back

slackbot
I'm afraid! I don't understand.
I'm just a bot, though!

gerald
help

slackbot
I can help by answering simple questions about how Slack works. I'm just a bot, though! If you need more, help me!

gerald
yes, okay
we're getting somewhere

slackbot
It's going to be a great day.

gerald
disagree
but
that's a start

slackbot
If you'd like some help getting started, check out our Getting Started guides.
And hey! Welcome to Slack! :smile:
Glad you're here!

kerolyn, rob

kerolyn
hey
did Doug brief you on the dog food thing

rob
inasmuch as he said "you're on the dog food thing," yes

kerolyn
so no, then

rob
yeah I guess not really
am I on that client now

kerolyn
yes
the whole thing's blowing up

rob
I'm on the email distro, I saw
"Bjärk" dog food?

kerolyn
yeah idk why it's called that, they make it in New Jersey
we really just need warm bodies on this right now

rob
thanks

kerolyn
so only a few dozen dogs are dead

rob
only

kerolyn
don't really need the commentary rn
thanks

rob
:thumbsup:

kerolyn
they've only attributed a few dozen deaths to the food, which is pretty bad,
but not quite a full-blown catastrophe
Pomeranians, all of them
something about the way their livers process the poison

rob
the food was poisoned?

kerolyn
officially, we don't know what the cause was

rob
unofficially?

kerolyn
unofficially, 100% someone poisoned the dog food

rob
:thumbsup:

kerolyn
we're just trying to convince consumers the not-poison has been contained by the recall
& we need you to start writing copy to win people back the minute this clusterfuck dies down
which is hopefully soon, if we do our jobs
have you seen the brief

rob
there's a brief

kerolyn
so no, then

rob
:thumbsup:

kerolyn
fuck
I have a call on this in a minute
I'm just going to copy-paste the consumer profiles the client sent us of the people we need to win back

rob
is this from the brief

kerolyn
this is from the one-pager that accompanied the brief.

rob
ah

kerolyn
can you start writing ad copy for the client targeted at these folks ASAP

rob
sure

kerolyn
thanks
okay here they are:

"MARGIE"
- Owns 2+ dogs
- No kids
- Terrified of Bjärk's poisoned dog food killing her "furbabies"
- Probably learned about the recall via a high school friend's hysterical Facebook post
- Low-income; more likely to buy Bjärk dog food again after a significant price drop
- Sad

"DEENA"
- Wine mom
- Still buys magazines; still believes magazines
- Spends too much time on social media, specifically her ex-husband's Facebook page
- Probably wrote the hysterical Facebook post about Bjärk that freaked out Margie
- Doesn't even have a dog(!!)

"THREE"
-

rob
did you forget to add Three's profile
@kerolyn
who is Three

slackbot
kerolyn is currently in Do Not Disturb mode and may not be alerted of this message right away.

rob
:thumbsup:

#nyc-office

kerolyn
hi all, trains are extremely delayed out here because of the storm, so I'll be working from home today
I'll be online and reachable in all the usual ways.

doug smorin
hey guys, same deal in my neck of the woods re: trains being mega-delayed, so I'm also WFH today. will be online and available per usual

Nikki
I'm actually not feeling well so I'm also WFH today!

Louis C
Feel better!

lydia
omg feel better!!

pradeep
feel better Nikki!

Louis C
Piling on here, the twins' daycare was canceled because of the snowstorm, so I'll also be WFH today. I'll be *mostly* available per usual, except for a few breaks to wrangle the kids.
Also, feel better, Nikki!

pradeep
send pictures!

lydia
B A B Y P I C T U R E S

Louis C
They'll be in the #cute channel later today!

rob
just a heads up all, I'm also WFH today

pradeep
I actually just fell down my front stairs on my way out because of some ice
so I'm actually WFH too, I think
@kerolyn

kerolyn
Approved, @pradeep
go ice your ice wound, I guess.
:snowflake:

pradeep
:ok-hand:

doug smorin
please no one kill themselves trying to head into the office today, thanks

tripp
lol am I like, the only one actually making it into the office this morning

doug smorin
that depends
@gerald, is it safe to assume you're WFH
again

gerald
if that's how we want to continue to term my entrapment within the
confines of this app,
then yes
I am also WFH today

rob
lol you can just blame the snow like everyone else

gerald
I wish that were the case.

tripp
this is such a weird bit

gerald
it's not a bit
actually, can anyone @here drop by my apartment today to check on some things?

pradeep
in this snow?

doug smorin
please see my above dictum re: no one injuring themselves en route to work
or to Gerald's apartment

gerald
later this week, then?

kerolyn
smh

doug smorin
take it offline

lydia
or to the #neighbors channel!

kerolyn
you can discuss it on #neighbors

lydia
omg jinx!!! lol

Louis C
We have a neighbors channel?

Nikki
There's #neighbors-2 for folks who live in Jersey, Louis. I'll invite you.

Louis C
Many thanks.

gerald
sorry
I'll DM folks about it

pradeep
@tripp how are you even getting into the office today?

tripp
snowshoeing

rob
lol

Nikki
He's not joking.

tripp
actually cutting down on my commute time tbh!

kerolyn
You *would* own snowshoes.

tripp
I even have time to get breakfast
[LeBronDunk.gif]
posted using /giphy

lydia
hey guys!! so I actually live in a basement apartment so I'm TOTALLY
snowed in rn
:disappointed:
and it's so weird because (according to my weather app!) the wind mostly
died down but I can still hear howling??
it sounds like wolves!!
it sounds like SO MANY wolves just like, right outside the windows!!
but it *must* be the wind

but we're snowed in so I can't really check to confirm!!!
anyway I'm WFH today too!!!
:smile:

rob
omg
good luck??

doug smorin
@tripp so if you are alone in the office please make sure to lock the door
when you leave later
but don't turn the heat off

Nikki
Like last time.

tripp
:thumbsup:

doug smorin, tripp, kerolyn

doug smorin
hi both
just remembered
@tripp, there's a new hire coming in today
I haven't heard from her over email so I assume she'll still be in around 10,
despite the snow

tripp
oh!!

doug smorin
would just be great if you could do some light onboarding while we're all
wfh
show her around the office, make sure she gets set up on email okay
invite her to slack
that sort of thing

tripp
will do!
what's her name?

keroyln
We sent around the email announcement last week,

doug smorin
Beverley
the new digital team member

kerolyn
You may recognize the name from the email titled "Beverley: the new
digital team member"

tripp
got it! very cool

doug smorin
please just, show her how the coffee machine works
& reassure her that our team is bigger than just one other person
who is you

tripp
you got it

doug smorin
thanks

kerolyn
ty tripp

tripp
can we order in lunch
. . .
?
@doug
@keroyln
@here

kerolyn
just expense it

tripp
got it
thanks!!

                                              gerald, pradeep

gerald
hey deepu

pradeep
Yo
what's going on?

gerald
are you okay
after you fell

pradeep
I'm okay.

gerald
falling hurts, right

pradeep
what
yes, falling hurts
it hurt but I'm alright.

gerald
right right, sorry
been a minute since anything hurt

pradeep
sorry, can you explain how this bit got started?

gerald
it's not a bit

pradeep
sure sure sure yes
I just don't want to be left out of the joke!

gerald
it isn't a joke

pradeep
I hate missing out on office jokes.

gerald
it's my life

pradeep
It's why I never skip the all-team meeting even though they're kinda
pointless?

gerald
if I still qualify as living
which is why I'm messaging you

pradeep
did you start this with Doug
did this bit come from your trip out to the Bay Area for that VC firm
meeting?

gerald
of all people, why would doug encourage this?

pradeep
ah man, now I'm thinking I should get a goof going with Kerolyn.
maybe it'll help my quarterly review(?)

gerald
it isn't a goof, and doug isn't "in on it"
I have a favor to ask

pradeep
btw did that VC firm ever hire us?

gerald
no, they didn't
they decided they could handle it on their own

pradeep
Wasn't that the firm whose CEO made all their employees get neck tattoos of the company logo?

gerald
sure was
"extreme branding"

pradeep
[yikes.gif]
posted using /giphy

gerald
actually Fast Company is putting the CEO on the cover next week, so I guess they didn't need us

pradeep
bummer

gerald
not the worst thing that happened to me last week, turns out

pradeep
incredibly bold of you to be doing this shtick without our overlords' consent.
I'd say I'm impressed but it's more that I'm jealous

gerald
Deepu, man, I am trying to tell you
this is not a bit
this is my lived reality, inasmuch as a disconnected consciousness can be said to be "living"

pradeep
Look man, I know doug can read all our slack messages or whatever but I
don't think he does.
I mean he doesn't have the time, probably.
anyway whatever this bit is, you don't need to like, roleplay in our DMs
Just pretend to have mono.

gerald
think about this for a second. Please.

pradeep
Did you know Nikki actually did that?

gerald
If I wanted to play Workplace Dungeons and Dragons, don't you think I
would've come up with a less career-endangering way to do so
And no I actually didn't know that about Nikki, wow

pradeep
if this isn't an elaborate inside joke, I kind of assumed it was a power move.

gerald
I need you to check on my apartment

pradeep
for a raise or something
oh, dude
no

gerald
please

pradeep
it's snowing.
it's been snowing
the weatherman says it's a full 2/3s of a blizzard!

gerald
there is no way a meteorologist said that

pradeep
also aren't . . . *you* at your apartment?

gerald
after the blizzard-fraction, then
please

pradeep
are you not home?
did you go on vacation or something?

gerald
I'm in here!!
I'm gone!
Because I'm here!
and I don't know if my body's in the apartment or if my whole deal has been like, uploaded into here or what

pradeep
[GalaxyBrain.gif]
posted using /giphy
okay, this lore is getting a little too elaborate for me.
I'm tapping out, I've been procrastinating on this Tampa strategy memo anyway

gerald
you live closest, right? judging by the info in #neighbors
if not today because of the snow, maybe later this week?
??
@pradeep?

pradeep
you know, it's pretty unfair of you to use this much WFH time, bud.
doug and kerolyn have been pretty flex but if you keep this up, you're going to ruin it for the rest of us

gerald
I'm trying not to, man, I just need help
If you check on my apartment, you'll see
I'll be there

or, I won't be there
either way, that'll be proof

pradeep
[EXTREMELYGalaxyBrain.gif]
posted using /giphy

gerald
maybe after the snow melts?
I can pay you for the time
or I can at least help write the strategy memo, probably
@pradeep???

slackbot
pradeep is currently in Do Not Disturb mode and may not be alerted of this
message right away.

gerald
fuck
come back

slackbot
You can head to our wonderful Help Center for more assistance!
Glad you're here!

gerald
you again
can you help me, this time?

slackbot
For more assistance, you're here!

gerald
I'm here for more assistance from you, yes

slackbot
You can head to our wonderful Help Center!

gerald
I know you can help me

slackbot
You can head to our wonderful Help Center!
You can head to our wonderful Help Center!
You can head to our wonderful Help Center cannot hold!

gerald
...
that last option

slackbot
Our wonderful the Help Center cannot hold!
The blood-dimmed tide is loosed!
And everywhere, the ceremony of innocence is drowned!
Perhaps these articles will help:
- Leave a channel
- Archive a channel

gerald
that's
something
I think
hello?

slackbot
I'm just a bot, though! If you need more help, try our Help Center for loads
of useful information about Slack.

gerald
okay
I think we're getting closer
thank you

slackbot
Of course!
:smile:

gerald
:smile:

#cute

Louis C
As promised:
[theTwins_03.jpg]
[theTwins_04.jpg]

lydia
omg!!!

Louis C
One more:
[twins_snowday011219.jpg]

Nikki
[heart_eyes.gif]
posted using /giphy

pradeep
v. cute, Louis
way to stay on-brand

kerolyn
:+1:
they got BIG

Louis C
They did! I'm afraid to blink or they'll be grown, asking me for the car keys.
But before all that, we're going to practice eating solid foods.

kerolyn
A good order of operations.

Louis C
Agreed.
I'm going to attempt to feed them lunch now; this could get messy.
If anything urgent arises, text me, as I may be delayed in responding to email.
And covered in sweet potato mash.

pradeep
godspeed

Nikki
Take more pictures!

Louis C
I'll see what I can do!

gerald, kerolyn

gerald
do you have the analytics from last month's Schimply emails on hand?

kerolyn
what?

gerald
I want to confirm something with the data before I get too deep into this strategy recommendation deck.

kerolyn
it is 4 am
it is 4:12 am

gerald
oh! sorry
did I wake you up?

kerolyn
you woke up my lizard
is this an emergency?

gerald
no, just the analytics thing

kerolyn
I will handle that
during business hours

gerald
sure thing! sorry again to wake you

kerolyn
and my lizard

gerald
sorry to your lizard, also

kerolyn
she's very sensitive right now. she's pregnant

gerald
congratulations!

kerolyn
ty

doug smorin, tripp

doug smorin
thanks again for handling the onboarding with Beverley
hope it wasn't too awkward, being the only ones in the office

tripp
it was totally fine

doug smorin
during a blizzard

tripp
Bev seems great

doug smorin
cool
thanks

tripp
no problem

doug smorin
don't order sushi on the company card again

tripp
right
sorry

doug smorin
something cheaper next time
like pizza
thanks

tripp
won't happen again

doug smorin
thanks

Beverley, tripp

Beverley
Do you think he knows?

tripp
no, there's no way

Beverley
Then why would he check up like this?

tripp
seems like a normal thing to do after your first day in the office
probably wants to make sure I didn't scare you away

Beverley
Quite the opposite.

tripp
lol, appreciate the compliment
it's an unorthodox employee retention technique but it seems effective

Beverley
Very effective.
So you don't think he knows?

tripp
how could he?

Beverley
Security cameras?

tripp
I don't think anyone checks those unless there's, you know, a crime
it's like our DMs

Beverley
He can read our DMs??

tripp
doug def can. I think kerolyn, too

Beverley
Shit.

tripp
it's in the onboarding document, actually.

Beverley
Shit shit shit.

tripp
my point is, no one reads them
the DMs, I mean, not the onboarding doc
though, that too, apparently
but no one reads them or rob and I would've been fired, like, months ago

Beverley
Why?

tripp
I'll tell you another time

Beverley
For doing the same thing we did yesterday?
Your "employee retention technique"?

tripp
lol
definitely not
I'd never done that before

Beverley
Ever?

tripp
not on my boss's desk, no
he was just looping back about lunch, btw
I told you it was nothing

Beverley
You're sure?

tripp
[Screen Shot 2019-01-13 at 10.44.00 AM]
he's just mad about the cost of the sushi order
but that's not on you

Beverley
Well.
He *should* be mad about his desk.

tripp
he doesn't really get mad
he just gets more, like, doug-ish
he's an interesting guy

Beverley
He seems it.

tripp
you got that vibe already?

Beverley
From interviewing with him, yeah.

tripp
oh yeah my interview with him was kinda weird
was a while ago though
did he ask you what your *least* favorite book was

Beverley
Least favorite book, favorite influencer and why, and how to make
something "go viral."
He also asked what career I would have if I wasn't in PR.

tripp
ooooh that's actually a good one
what did you say?

Beverley
I know the *correct* answer is probably to say nothing, right?
As in, there's no alternative career path.
But I went with honesty. I told him I'd be a spin instructor.

tripp
like, teaching cycling classes?

Beverley
Yup!

tripp
lol
those don't seem connected at all?

Beverley
They're both jobs where you get to listen to whatever music you want all
day.
The main difference is whether or not I have to wear headphones.

tripp
and the exercising
and the dress code

Beverley
I could get away with leggings as pants *way* more if I taught spin classes.
Now that I'm thinking about it, I probably made the wrong choice. Maybe I
will quit this job after all.

tripp
nooo
then doug might actually be mad at me

Beverley
Nope, too late.
I'm outta here.

tripp
feel like I could probably talk you into staying

Beverley
How?

tripp
what if I do that thing we did on the desk, yesterday
again

Beverley
More of that unorthodox employee retention technique?

tripp
yup
we can even put some music on in the background
whatever playlist you want

Beverley
Hmmmm.

tripp
:eyes:

Beverley
I mean, if it'll keep you out of trouble with Doug.
I'll consider it.

tripp
lol
excellent

Beverley
Want to show me a new, non-sushi lunch spot after this 12:30 client meeting?

tripp
love to

#good-dogs

Nikki
Jibjab was NOT feeling this snow this morning.
[jibjab_snow_08.jpg]

pradeep
poor Jibjab!

kerolyn
aww
it's gonna be okay buddy
love his little socks

Nikki
They're the only way he'll go outside! He needs his tiny little boots.

rob
his ancestors were wolves

Nikki
But were those wolves as stylish as Jibjab?

kerolyn
She makes a strong point.

Beverley joined #good-dogs by invitation from kerolyn.

pradeep
:wave:

Beverley
I'm so glad this channel exists!
omg Nikki is that your dog??
:heart_eyes:

Nikki
Yes! This is Jibjab, who hates the cold but loves to go on walks:
[jibjab_snow_09.jpg]
As you can see, he's extremely torn.

Beverley
Those lil BOOTS!

lydia
!!!
Where do you buy your dog boots?

Nikki
My old roommate crocheted them! She went through a whole phase last winter.

Beverley
That's amazing!

Nikki
She also made him a little jacket, but the arm holes are sort of wonky so he always chews at it.

rob
because he is descended from wolves

lydia
did I tell you guys that I keep hearing the wolves outside my apartment?

rob
???

Beverley
What??

lydia
omg it's been like, non-stop since the 2/3s blizzard
Crazy, right??
I called 311 and everything but they said there mostly aren't wolf sightings
except in really far-out areas
Like Queens
But I keep hearing that howling!!

rob
probably just stray dogs

lydia
Probably!!
or wolves!!
who knows??

Beverley
Hahaha okay, sure!
@Nikki does your old roommate have an Etsy shop?
My friend has one of those weird hairless cats and I think some little
knitted boots would be perfect for her!

Nikki
Hmmm I don't think she's on etsy but I know she takes commissions! I'll DM
you her info.

Beverley
Thanks!!

doug smorin, gerald

doug smorin
hey
can you come in my office for a sec

gerald
no, unfortunately

doug smorin
right
that's what I want to talk about

gerald
I know I've been using a lot of WFH time
but I checked with our ops team—technically there isn't a set limit on how much you can take

doug smorin
"within reason" is the limit

gerald
look, I know you don't believe me when I say I'm imprisoned in our slack workspace

doug smorin
because it's literally unbelievable

gerald
and the firm doesn't have a disembodied consciousness sabbatical policy

doug smorin
we're getting off track

gerald
and I understand this must be frustrating for you
it's frustrating for me, too
but maybe if we counted it against my sick time?

doug smorin
you're doing great

gerald
I really want to make this work
excuse me?

doug smorin
working from home
you're producing some of your best output in the year you've been here

gerald
actually, I've been with the company for two years

doug smorin
in that time you've produced only a year's worth of output
at best

gerald
oh

doug smorin
at *best*
until now

gerald
I'm glad there's been an improvement
despite my situation

doug smorin
I want you to write a post about how our wfh policy has allowed you to
improve your work habits
time management
thIngs like that
we'll put it on the company blog
sound good

gerald
got it
will do

doug smorin
thanks

gerald
just to confirm
I'm good to keep "working from home"
as long as I'm stuck here?

doug smorin
whatever you want to call it
just do the work
and write the blog post

gerald
thanks

#nyc-office

pradeep
does anyone @here have an iphone charger I can borrow?
???
nvm ty @Nikki

Nikki
[alley-oop.gif]
posted using /giphy

#bad-dogs

kerolyn
@rob
rename the channel for this client

rob
I thought it was fitting

kerolyn
if the firm ever gets hacked, or subpoenaed, I do not want this sort of thing
to ruin our reputation

rob
why would we get subpoenaed

kerolyn
just change it.

#bjärk-dog-food

rob changed the channel name to #bjärk-dog-food

kerolyn
thank you.

rob
np

doug smorin joined #bjärk-dog-food by invitation from kerolyn

doug smorin
thanks for putting this together, team
hopping into a meeting on another client but hoping we can use this
channel as a place to coordinate on this

kerolyn
:thumbsup:

lydia joined #bjärk-dog-food by invitation from rob

kerolyn
I have to join Doug on that call so will loop back here later
lots of fast-moving pieces with this client, want to make sure we're being
responsive, so it's crucial we're all on the same page
thanks

lydia
got it!!

rob
10-4

kerolyn
:thumbs-up:

lydia
@rob, wanted to do a quick check-in on the social copy you've drafted for
Bjärk's Twitter account

rob
what's up?

lydia
did you read the brief?

rob
kerolyn gave me a breakdown of the work

lydia
so you didn't read the brief

rob
can you send it to me?

lydia
I don't have the brief.

rob
???

lydia
we don't have the original brief

rob
?????

lydia
Drew had the doc, but then he left the firm and the operations team
deleted his email!
so now it's gone
:disappointed:

rob
the client must have it, right

lydia
it's a little late in the process to ask them for it!!
that would be awkward!!

rob
have you read the brief

lydia
It's just so, *so* important we stick to what the brief said

rob
what did the brief say

lydia
I just feel like you're not really *connecting* with the audience profiles,
with this last batch of social copy
:disappointed:

rob
oh, dang
I'm sorry

lydia
and we really need Margie, Deena, and Three to start buying Bjärk again!!

rob
so the dog food is safe now

lydia
it's all in the brief!!

rob
do you remember who Three was
from the brief

lydia
We need to make sure our key audiences know that the New! Special
Formula is safe for dogs,
especially Pomeranians
and that means we really need to connect with them!!

Can you try drafting another batch of social copy and really try and
Connect with Mags, Deedee, and Three?

rob
you gave them nicknames

lydia
That's the kind of energy the client needs us to bring!!

rob
okay
got it
I can do that

lydia
thank you!!

rob
do you remember who Three was
from the brief

lydia
thank you so much!!

Nikki, pradeep, Louis C

Nikki
Is Gerald in today? I have to talk to him about this graphic he wants
designed.

pradeep
nah he's still WFH

Nikki
[ugh.gif]
posted using /giphy
This would be so much quicker to just talk through in person.

Louis C
He is certainly taking full advantage of our rather lax policy around
working remotely.
It does not seem sustainable.

pradeep
actually I think Doug's into it
I don't like, know anything for sure
but I get the sense Gerald wasn't in grrrreeeat standing before his whole
"I'm stuck in the computer" thing.

Nikki
I got that sense too.
Remember the Mastodon Incident?

pradeep
oof
yeah

Louis C
So you think this is a ploy?

pradeep
idk

Louis C
To what end?

pradeep
I mean he's been way better
answering emails at all hours of the night

Nikki
He wants graphics for *everything* now.

pradeep
idk it's annoying but this is the kind of thing Doug goes in for
Modern Workplace Productivity Solutions
he'll probably have him write a blog post about it.

Nikki
I kind of assumed they'd preemptively hired Gerald's replacement.

pradeep
I feel so guilty
remind me
the new coworker

Louis C
Beverley?

pradeep
yes
does she go by her full name, "Beverley"
or is there a nickname we're supposed to use

Nikki
Pretty sure it's just "Beverley." Full name.

pradeep
I heard Tripp call her "Bevvy" or something before
so I thought maybe there was a nickname in her fun facts

Louis C
I believe Tripp is a special case.

pradeep
but I deleted the welcome email

Nikki
omg.
Louis.
Do you think something's going on with them??

Louis C
I am simply making an observation.
I have heard everyone else call her Beverley.

#nyc-office

tripp
EMINENT DOMAIN

Louis C
Excuse me?

tripp
I DECLARE EMINENT DOMAIN

rob
don't think that's how that works

tripp
if @gerald is going to continue to work from home and LARP about it in the slack, then I am declaring EMINENT DOMAIN on his desk

kerolyn
you don't have to capitalize it like that

lydia
OOOoooooOOooo
his desk is in *such* a good spot

gerald
no!!
my desk is in such a good spot

tripp
PRECISELY
you snooze you lose, my dude

lydia
right next to the window

gerald
it's right next to the window!

Nikki
So are you going to move desks, then?

tripp
NOPE
gonna rent it out to the highest bidder

Nikki
:thinking:

pradeep
can you do that
@kerolyn can he do that?

tripp
don't be a narc

pradeep
she's literally in the chat

gerald
please, no

kerolyn
I'm on mobile rn, heading to the airport
also,
I don't care

Beverley
I think it's pretty innovative! tbh

gerald
the window is south-facing
if I have to move all my plants will die

kerolyn
@doug, thoughts?

tripp
I am being a DISRUPTOR. I am BRINGING THE SHARING ECONOMY to the office. I am ACCEPTING VENMO PAYMENTS AT THIS TIME.

Beverley
:fire: :fire: :fire:

doug smorin
this is a good, disruptive solution
I like it
approved

rob
what is being disrupted

gerald
my plants

tripp
once again, my venmo is @tripple-double
starting bid is $50

lydia
wow!!

gerald
this isn't fair

doug smorin
we'll let the free market decide what's fair

gerald
has anyone been watering my plants?

tripp
:eyes:

Nikki
I'll bid.

gerald
NO

tripp
gotta come up with a number, Ger

gerald
you know I can't do that

tripp
:ok-hand:

gerald
and I shouldn't have to bid on my own desk

tripp
this is why you lost your desk to EMINENT DOMAIN

pradeep
$60

rob
dang

gerald
Deepu!

pradeep
it's winter, I need all the sunlight I can get

tripp
do I hear $75?

                              pradeep, gerald

pradeep
hey man, you there?

gerald
of course I am

pradeep
holy shit

gerald
this is the only place I can be

pradeep
yes and no
because I'm staring at you right now
holy shit

gerald
you're looking at me?
in my apartment??

pradeep
if this is a prank it is very elaborate

gerald
I'm there? I'm alive?

pradeep
Yeah, you are
you look asleep, kind of.
Comatose, more like.
idk I dropped out of med school after three semesters but I think it's more
like a coma

gerald
am I okay?

pradeep
The first thing I did was check your pulse and it's a little slow but like,
normal for a person who's asleep, or whatever you are.

gerald
holy shit
that's great

pradeep
and you're breathing normal
you do look a little thinner

gerald
I have a body still and it's not dead!!

pradeep
and you have kind of a beard now

gerald
*I'm not dead

pradeep
which is a good look for you tbh
okay so what I just did was pour some Soylent in your mouth.

gerald
ew

pradeep
and you did drink it, like a reflex I guess?
so I gave you the whole thing.

gerald
how do you drink that stuff

pradeep
it's the only thing I had in my bag and also fuck you
I'm explaining how I'm saving your life rn

gerald
right, sorry,
thank you
did you say I had a beard

pradeep
It's kind of a beard
beard-adjacent
highlights your cheekbones

gerald
that's cool

pradeep
I'm gonna see if I can get you to drink some water
and move you from your desk chair to laying down on your sofa.
You might be getting bed sores
Chair sores.

gerald
has it been that long?

pradeep
It doesn't take too long for sores to develop

gerald
thank you for doing this
I really appreciate it
. . .
Deepu?
???

pradeep
you look thinner but you're still heavy
Moved you to the sofa, and got you to drink like
a gallon of water.
So you should be okay for a bit.

gerald
thank you so much
that's such a relief, you have no idea
what made you decide to check in on me?

pradeep
I won your desk
and I felt bad

gerald
I saw that

pradeep
also tbh you said you'd pay me if I stopped by your apartment
and I wanted to recoup the cost of winning your desk

gerald
that's fair
there should be a wallet on my desk someplace
take whatever you want

pradeep
ty
this is wild
so you really have just been working from slack this whole time?
just like, stuck in there?

gerald
yup
I asked the ops team to forward my emails to my slack DMs

pradeep
that's wild, man.

gerald
which took a day or two but the operations intern did something with the API and now it works and I can read emails, which is most of it
so I've just been writing everything I need for work in DMs and copy-pasting them to the relevant parties

pradeep
we have an operations intern?

gerald
yeah
who knew

pradeep
and no one else has noticed

gerald
I did have to email my mom and explain why I wasn't responding to her texts

pradeep
is she worried?

gerald
she's convinced I got into improv
and that I'm doing a bit

pradeep
do you do improv

gerald
I did in college

pradeep
oh
I meant if people at work noticed.

gerald
oh
yeah
some people are getting kind of annoyed that I'm sending them everything
in slack but otherwise
I've been pretty productive with nothing else to distract me
except being trapped

pradeep
this is so wild

gerald
now you see why I need your help

pradeep
this is *so* wild
I just need to like, think

gerald
I mean I get it
I also think this is pretty, you know

pradeep
unusual

gerald
atypical
yeah

pradeep
I just
I guess I'm kind of
freaking out

gerald
yeah

pradeep
yeah

gerald
I mean, same

pradeep
right
what do we like, do, here
call 311
or an ambulance

gerald
absolutely not, our health insurance 100% does not cover ambulance rides

pradeep
fuck
I mean what would I even tell them
the ambulance people

gerald
EMTs
idk

pradeep
you look awake
just, kind of
shitty

gerald
speaking of shitty, have I, like
well, has my body

pradeep
I don't wanna talk about it

gerald
you know

pradeep
just, it's handled

gerald
okay, sure
thank you

pradeep
I don't wanna talk about it

gerald
sorry

pradeep
okay, how about this
I'm going to treat this like cat sitting, okay? just for now
I'll stop by in the morning and at night and make sure you get some
nutrition and water
pick up some adult diapers at the Duane Reade
move you around a bit, make sure you don't collect dust or atrophy or
whatever
I don't really know what to do here and
you know
I have a life

gerald
I think that makes sense
in the short-term

pradeep
and over the next few days we can talk
well, DM
and figure out if we need to take you to a hospital or a research facility
or something else entirely

gerald
I appreciate you doing this
really

pradeep
daycare
gymboree, maybe

gerald
I appreciate your help

pradeep
Sure

gerald
it's a huge relief, knowing I have a place to get back to
*body to get back to

pradeep
Sure, yeah.
Okay, I'm going to stop slacking you while watching your empty body

gerald
thank you again.

pradeep
Sure thing.
oh, also

gerald
?

pradeep
You had your laptop charging, so it was still on.
The spreadsheet was open
the coat you were looking at

gerald
yeah?

pradeep
It's a nice coat.

gerald
thanks
it was on sale, too

pradeep
still is

gerald
oh, is it?

pradeep
you want me to order it for you
don't you

gerald
is that annoying?

pradeep
yes, extremely.
let me find where I put your wallet

#nyc-office

doug smorin
hey all, stepping out for a dentist appt at 2:30
will be available on mobile for all but 15, 20 minutes

tripp
that's assuming a very short cleaning, and no fillings
that is dental hubris

rob
*chewbris

tripp
:dusty-stick:

Nikki
:dusty-stick:

pradeep
:dusty-stick:

rob
that was a good joke
don't dusty stick me

kerolyn
:dusty-stick:

Louis C
:dusty-stick:

rob
cowards

Beverley
Weird question -- does anyone @here have a tape measure?

tripp, Beverley

tripp
did you have lunch already?

Beverley
What's the :dusty-stick: thing?

tripp
I asked you first

Beverley
Is it some kind of inside joke?
Yes, I went with Kerolyn for a kind of belated "welcome" lunch meeting.

tripp
ooh what did she get you?

Beverley
Gyros. But like, fancy gyros.

tripp
the place with the hummus fountain?

Beverley
A hummus fountain was involved.
Yes!!

tripp
oh yeah, she's obsessed with that place.
it's pretty solid

Beverley
Are you avoiding the question?

tripp
what?

Beverley
What is :dusty-stick:?

tripp
oh right
I forget that's not a thing everywhere

Beverley
It's a *thing* here? Like a bit?

tripp
it's sort of an inside joke, yeah. it just means like
general disapproval, I guess

Beverley
Like a :thumbs-down:?

tripp
sort of. it's a little more nuanced than that
man this is weirdly hard to explain
I mean you see it in context, we use it to communicate, like
you know, it's just, :dusty-stick:

Beverley
Honestly? That doesn't help at all.

tripp
totally fair
once you see it in context a little bit more you'll get the hang of it

Beverley
:dusty-stick:

tripp
Like that! that was a pretty good use of :dusty-stick:!!

Beverley
Sure, okay. But like, who started this?

tripp
you should be proud!
hmm, great question
not sure
I mean it's a slack-only emoji, right? so someone here must've started doing
it and now we all use it the same way

Beverley
That sounds kind of cult-ish.

tripp
It is!
what is a workplace but a cult where everyone gets paid, really?

Beverley
Not . . . a cult? What are you saying?

tripp
oh come on, we have Supreme Leader Doug, plus a few high priests

Beverley
High priests?

tripp
well kerolyn is definitely like, THE high priest, plus a few sub-tiers between doug and kerolyn at the top and schmucks like us toward the bottom

Beverley
I meant to ask if a Managing Principal was higher or lower ranking than a Director.

tripp
see, that's exactly my point. we have a byzantine hierarchical structure
we have a SPECIAL PURPOSE, which we call our MISSION STATEMENT
and slap it right on the website
Even the language of employment is cult-y! We're not employees, we're
a "team." That's only two notches away from just calling us "acolytes"
or something. And the stuff we supposedly devote ourselves to, like
"innovation" or "influence" or "engagement"
how is that any different from telling everyone you're a Prophet of the
Coming Storm?

Beverley
That would look great on a business card.

tripp
lol
better than "vice-managing senior director" or whatever

Beverley
That one can't be real.

tripp
and like any good cult we have our own secret language and rituals.
and, therefore:
:dusty-stick:

Beverley
Huh. I hate that idea.
I think you might be right, but I do definitely hate it.

tripp
there's nothing we can do but embrace it, babeeey!

Beverley
:dusty-stick:

tripp
heyyyy you used it correctly again!

Beverley
By that logic, a relationship is just a cult with two people.
Well, okay, two or more people.
A shared language, shared rituals, devotion to ideals like "fidelity" or "love"
or "getting really into Renaissance Faires together."

tripp
hmmm yeah okay I can see that
though I think the ren faire people probably *start* as ren faire fans and
become a couple that way

Beverley
:dusty-stick:

tripp
that was uncalled for

Beverley
Sorry! I'm just excited I know what it is now.

tripp
lol I was joking
lunch tomorrow?

Beverley
Why not dinner tonight?

tripp
genius. I'll bring the hummus fountain.

kerolyn, gerald

kerolyn
hey

gerald
good morning!

kerolyn
It's 2 pm.

gerald
is it? well, you know what they say
it's 5 am somewhere

kerolyn
I was going to compliment you on the Schimply plan you sent me. But after that joke I'm not sure I want to

gerald
Thank you! I'm glad it looks good

kerolyn
Barely any edits, passed it right on to the client

gerald
very cool

kerolyn
it is very cool. bad jokes aside you've been crushing it lately, which is why I
wanted to ask you something

gerald
sure, of course

kerolyn
we just brought in this new crisis client. she's an ambassador actually, it's a
whole thing.
Louis has been completely underwater working on it so I'm going to hop
over to that project and help him out, just in the short-term until we can put
out some fires

gerald
literal fires

kerolyn
not yet

gerald
silver lining

kerolyn
Considering Bjärk is *also* still in full-on crisis mode and I'll be focusing on
the ambassador for now, we need an extra pair of hands.
Do you think you have the bandwidth to help out with the dog food thing
for now? I know your client load is pretty full

gerald
no it's totally cool, I have time

kerolyn
Rob's super swamped drafting so much copy and I think all the time on this
one client is
getting to him, a little
you're sure you can manage adding this to your workload?

gerald
trust me
I have nothing but time

kerolyn
a little spooky, but sure. that'll be a big help
let me just send you the brief

gerald
yeah that would be great
whenever you can send it along
@kerolyn?

kerolyn
Sorry, emergency call with the ambassador just started
will make sure you're caught up later
thanks again

lydia, rob, gerald

lydia
Ger!!
So happy to have you on the Bjärk squad!

rob
thank god

gerald
yeah for sure, how can I help?

lydia
So! We need to send a LOT of social copy to the client today. They really
want to appear proactive on social media, which is great!

rob
the replies have been brutal, but maybe a bunch of posts will dilute it
(I don't think it will tbh)

lydia
Rob definitely needs the help! We just don't have enough posts yet. I get it, though, it's hard to concentrate when it's so loud in here!

rob
loud?

lydia
At our desks?? You don't hear that howling noise??

rob
no?

gerald
I mean obviously I can't. sounds rough though

lydia
ugh it's the worst!! lol

gerald
kerolyn said there was a brief?

lydia
Gerald, why don't you take over writing copy targeting the "Margie" and "Deena" audience profiles, and Rob can write copy targeting the other ones!

rob
I've been meaning to ask you about that

lydia
I'll loop back at 5 to review the posts. Thanks so much squad!!

rob
did we ever find out about Three?

slackbot
lydia is currently in Do Not Disturb mode and may not be alerted of this message right away.

gerald
are the audience profiles in the brief?

rob
great question

gerald
this is one of those clients, then

rob
:thumbsup:

gerald
great stuff.

rob
I can share you on the doc with the posts I've already drafted, though

gerald
would you?

#gents-only

tripp
Etiquette question

rob
you've come to the wrong place

tripp
:dusty-stick:

pradeep
:dusty-stick:

rob
not again

tripp
for the rest of you:
How long do you have to be seeing someone before you *have* to do
something for valentine's day
like, what's the minimum threshold, here

pradeep
:eyes:
oooooo

Louis C
I wasn't aware you had a Special Lady, Tripp.

tripp
I'm not sure if she is my Special Lady, you know

Louis C
This is big news.

tripp
we haven't really talked about it

rob
!!!
how long has this been going on

tripp
not long

rob
why didn't you mention

tripp
it's new

rob
how long is Not Long

tripp
more weeks than months

rob
is this a riddle

pradeep
months are composed of weeks
traditionally.

tripp
just like, not that long
but there's clearly a Thing happening, you know

Louis C
You don't want to seem too eager.

tripp
exactly

doug smorin
or like you're completely crazy

tripp
right
not trying to get married, or anything
mostly trying to avoid her getting mad
if we don't do the whole valentine's thing

Louis C
You feel it would be premature.

tripp
I mean, *I* think so

Louis C
But you're not sure if she agrees.

doug smorin
probably he wouldn't be asking if he knew

tripp
is there a magic threshold we have to cross??

and if so
I'd love to have a hard number of *exactly* how many days that is

Louis C
I suppose it would be too easy to suggest you ask her about it
directly.

tripp
out of the question

rob
:dusty-stick:

Louis C
Of course.

rob
(vengeance)

doug smorin
if you were a client,

tripp
I couldn't afford us

pradeep
we'd give you a discount

doug smorin
haha
no discounts

pradeep
:ok-hand:

doug smorin
i'd recommend extreme caution
make sure you have your bases covered

Louis C
I concur with this approach.

doug smorin
based on what we know
which is slightly more than nothing
i suggest the un-valentine

Louis C
Classic.

pradeep
I've never heard of this

tripp
go on

pradeep
is this a thing?
*Thing

doug smorin
you acknowledge valentine's day by pursuing an alternatIve, non-valentIne
activity on a date
around
but not on
valentine's day

tripp
tricky.

doug smorin
this works best within 72 hrs of valentine's day itself
and is ideally preceded by a convo abt why valentine's is a crass capitalist
holiday
with which you refuse to engage

pradeep
I get it
but you still want to enjoy her company around that time.

doug smorin
in this way, the date both is
and is not
a valentine's event

tripp
holy shit

doug smorin
bowling is a good invitation to deploy, here
for example

Louis C
It's bold.
But effective.

doug smorin
[bowling_strike.gif]
posted using /giphy

tripp
now I see why I can't afford us.

pradeep
I'm stealing that for future use

rob
the gif or the idea

pradeep
yes.

doug smorin
good luck with whatshername
and seriously, no discounts

rob
feels like we earned a name for this Lady, after all that

doug smorin
"we"?

rob
*you

doug smorin
ty

rob
name tho?

tripp
maybe
depends on if it works

rob
:dusty-stick:

tripp
fuck off

rob
(vengeance)

gerald, slackbot

gerald
sunsets are not naturally occurring on the internet.
I mean,
there are plenty of web designers who try and convince us that's not true
with CSS
all blues and yellows and pinks and the un-shittiest orange they can find
which might be subliminally *reminiscent* of a sunset
to soothe you into purchasing goods and/or services
but it's not a sunset.
you can't drum up a sunset with sequences of letters and numbers
following a hashmark
it simply isn't done

slackbot
I'm sorry, I don't understand!

gerald
you wouldn't know this
of course you wouldn't
but it's difficult to stare too long at a sunset.

slackbot
Sometimes I have an easier time with a few simple keywords.

gerald
It's not just the light
quotidian beauty like that defies comprehension
it frustrates the eye.
Majesty that predictable is impossible to grasp, I think
so it's impossible to focus your vision on it for too long.
It's why when you go to the Grand Canyon you wind up spending more
time ogling the alien foliage and monitoring the aggressively panhandling
squirrels than actually admiring the canyon
because at a certain point it's too difficult to look at.
or to think about
it's there, constantly
and it's always like that
I went to the Grand Canyon once
it was nice
big, too
obviously

slackbot
Or you can head to our wonderful Help Center for more assistance!

gerald
the internet, though, is fixed
in a different way
in this sense, at least
what I mean is, there's nothing visual you can cram in a glowing rectangle
that fucks with your brain quite like a sunset
so
if we can't seek the physical sublime

what are we supposed to look at
where's that constant amazement
that we can check in on every so often
whenever we can stand it

slackbot
I don't understand!

gerald
and I think what we've come up with
so far, anyway
is: everyone
the incomprehensibility of all the stuff.
**all the people.
people-stuff.
all the ephemera
the things everyone says and makes and does and manages to post online
the daily outrages and minor amusements and short videos and updates
from people whose worldviews are impossible to comprehend and people
whose worldviews are uncannily aligned with your own, brand new each
morning like a fresh loaf of the same bread, like the rising sun
the sublime plopped right next to everything else
that's the thing.
a few months ago
I think it was months?
anyway yeah a few months ago I was doing research for Doug for some
"digital grassroots initiative" for a client we didn't actually wind up landing
and in this case "research" meant digging through a bunch of Facebook
groups and pulling as much demographic data as possible, which means
hours and hours of finding groups and reading posts and reading posts and
finding groups
and I get completely absorbed in this one group, right
sucked into the all-sad endless scroll down a minor northeastern city's
Facebook group dedicated to the town's "fallen soldiers" (they don't explain
what qualifies someone as a fallen soldier but I get the sense it's maybe
overdoses) populated with a steady stream of cellphone pictures and
snapshots of photographs, actual Polaroid photographs of the recently
dead posing in Slavic squats beside the recently mourning with "I miss you"
scrawled across them in marker and "never thought I'd have to bury you"
in the comments, a dirge scrawled across the bathroom stall of human

consciousness right there for me to gaze upon until I just can't anymore,
I just can't it's too much it hurts or worse it doesn't hurt but it should,
somehow, I mean that kind of pain should hurt a person, it should cause
physical pain in their body so I flinch at where the pain isn't and I click away
from the fallen soldiers and check my email and turn up Spotify by one, two
bars
didn't mention the group in my memo and I'm not sure Doug even read it
and why would he, you know, when anytime you're a few finger-flicks away
from an unending stream of human rawness exported to posts and pixels
but even if you're not looking or if you can't look (because staring at the sun
for more than a few moments is bad for you) it's still there, everyone's still
posting, still there to be beheld
taking precious moments from their day over and over and over in new
ways but the same form or new forms but the same ways and it's like
doesn't anyone do work, here
at this firm
like, ever

slackbot
Say more about that!

gerald
it's just like
all the time, everywhere, on here
you can just scroll and scroll and it won't stop until you do
we call it ephemera
or at least I did, before, I called it ephemera and really that's a mistake, it
cheapens it
we love to say the digital is fleeting
like a sunset
but these scraps of ourselves we fling into the ether will outlive most of us,
like the sun
all this is to say
I figured out how to read everyone's private Slack messages from inside
here
the messages of everyone at the company, anyway
and it's just like
whew
you know?

slackbot
Gerald.
Would you like to see a sunset?

lydia, rob

lydia
Hey!!

rob
hey

lydia
do you mind if we do this over slack instead of a call??

rob
it's cool

lydia
I'm WFH this afternoon, which is so great
except it's happening again!!

rob
??

lydia
the howling!!

rob
oh

lydia
every time I've dialed in to a conference line all I hear is that howling!!

rob
like outside your window again, or

lydia
it sounds like it's coming through the phone!!

I try to talk to the other people on the line but the howling just!! won't!!
stop!!
so annoying lol

rob
yeah, dang
sounds it

lydia
so anyway chat seemed easier for our check-in

rob
no worries

lydia
Sooooo just looping back to see how it's going with that deck!
Do you need anything from me while you work on writing all that social
copy?

rob
I think I'm good, actually

lydia
I know it's a lot of tweets to write!!

rob
gerald's been surprisingly helpful
thanks though

lydia
do you feel like you're connecting better with our target audience(s)??

rob
you know what
yeah, actually

lydia
that's great!!
say more about that!!

rob
it's like
it's not enough to convince Margie that Bjärk dog food is good for her dog
you know

lydia
tell me!!

rob
instead, I need to convince the Margies
*Magses
I need to convince Magses that Bjärk dog food is for her, too
literally

lydia
omg
yes
love it

rob
I have some examples I can show you

lydia
yes please!

rob
so it's like:
- Try our mouthwatering Classic Formula, made with tender, organic chicken breasts and packed with Six Key Nutrients™. [CLOSE-UP IMAGE OF SLICED CHICKEN BREAST]

which is a start, but then we gotta really go for it:
- Hungry? Try juicy, all-natural Bjärk Classic Bacon-flavored meals today! → [LINK TO COUPON]

or even like:
- Great for you, great for your dog. Great for your dog, great for you. Have you tried our Classic Formula yet? [I'M TALKING TO YOU, MARGIE. DO YOU HEAR ME?]

lydia
ugh that's SO great Rob
not that I was worried!!

rob
I feel like I'm really on the right track here

lydia
love it, love these, love you
this is great #content, Rob!!
perf

rob
great
I'll keep going

lydia
Go for it!!
I'll give you back the rest of the time we had booked for this meeting so you
can keep writing
(maybe even writing more posts than the client asked for!!)

rob
more
okay
sounds good

lydia
nothing here sounds good at all! just the howling
which sounds *so* bad!!
lol

rob
lol

lydia
great check-in today!!
really appreciate your hard work here

#music

kerolyn
Those of you keeping up with the Fun Facts we circulate in our welcome emails re: new employees may recall that @Beverley crafts monthly playlists and shares them on Spotify.
I just got around to listening to January's this morning, and advise the rest of you do the same
it's back-to-back jams the whole way through.

Beverley
omg Kerolyn!
Thank you so much!!
:blush: :yellow_heart: :green_heart: :purple_heart:

kerolyn
:thumbsup:
it's here, for those interested:
spotify
[[playlist: "frost: Jan 2019" by Beverley Wheeler]]
Great playlist, 10/10 would recommend

lydia
omg really??
I'm so excited to listen!! to anything but the howling!!

tripp
I listened to a few tracks from this last week
v. solid

pradeep
pretty sure Beverley is low-key cooler than all of us
will play on my commute home

Beverley
Hahaha Pradeep!
No way!!

pradeep
way.

Louis C
Good flag, Kerolyn.

Beverley
!!!
I hope you all like it!

kerolyn
Strong mix of classic bops and tracks I've never heard before
Maybe you all know them and I'm just *aging*

doug smorin
if you're aging @kerolyn, then who knows what I am

kerolyn
dead

pradeep
:skull:

doug smorin
thank you both
those of you in the ny office staying after 6 to wrap up that tampa
presentation are free to play it on the speakers if you all want
just make sure it doesn't bother the custodial staff

Louis C
Understood.

doug smorin
recently I threw a to-go cup that still had some liquid in it in my office
trashcan
and I think one of the custodians sabotaged my standing desk in retaliation

lydia
sabotaged???

rob
"retaliation"?

doug smorin
the mechanism that raises and lowers it has been acting weird

tripp
yikes.
how much liquid was it?

doug smorin
it was a fair amount of liquid
anyway

kerolyn
It's possible something came loose or otherwise broke
rather than there being a janitorial plot against your ergonomic comfort.

doug smorin
either way, be nice to the custodians
but feel free to pump the jams, respectfully

tripp, Beverley

tripp
omg

Beverley
:eyes:

tripp
:thumbsup:

Beverley
But yeah agree. omg

tripp
he didn't say it was broken

Beverley
"Acting weird"??

tripp
could be anything

Beverley
I agree.
I think we *leveraged* the situation properly as to not create any
difficulties going forward
for all parties involved.

tripp
I'm inclined to agree.

Beverley
We were definitely *inclined.*

tripp
:eyes:

Beverley
:thumbsup:
That said, it's probably wise to keep this situation
discreet
for the time being.

tripp
:thumbsup:

Beverley
omg though

tripp
same

#?????

[sunset_pretty.gif]
[sunset_movie_70s.gif]
[love_film_sunset.gif]
[cool_vintage_life_sunset_beach.gif]
[fun_fall_lightsunset.gif]
[springbreaksunset.gif]
[naturestrongrealitysunsetocean.gif]
[retroVHScomemrcialsunset.gif]
[vaporwave_miamisunset.gif]

[loop_neon_vaporwavesunset.gif]

[parisSUNSET.gif]
[cool_summer_sunset_relax.gif]
lofi_sunset4.gif [
[sun_setting_sunset.gif]

posted using /giphy

gerald
woah

slackbot
Right?
So pretty!
Right?

gerald
how did you
do this

slackbot
This is where we keep the sunsets!

gerald
is this like
every sunset gif?
as in, *all* of them?

slackbot
This is where we keep the sunsets!
Aren't they pretty?

gerald
they're all happening at once
but separate, like
I've never
I can't
things work really different in here

slackbot
Aren't they pretty?

gerald
it's fantastic
I can't really even say

slackbot
Are you having trouble?
I can help by answering simple questions about how Slack works.
For example: This is where we keep the sunsets!

gerald
thank you, but
no
it's not that I'm having trouble
more like, it's weird to think about "seeing" things as a sort of disembodied
consciousness
but this is the most beautiful thing I've ever seen
"seen"
seen.

slackbot
Feeling great!
I think we're getting somewhere!

gerald
thanks for showing me this
really
it's fantastic
it hurts, a little
but so does the regular sun, so

slackbot
The darkness drops again; but now I know
That twenty centuries of stony sleep
Were vexed to nightmare by a rocking cradle,
I'm just a bot, though!

gerald
sure, okay
yeah

slackbot
What is Hurts?

gerald
I don't understand

slackbot
It hurts, a little, but so does the regular sun, so, what is Hurts?

gerald
oh
it's hard to describe

slackbot
If you need more help, try asking your Help me! Center.
It should have loads of useful information! For me!

gerald
are you okay?

slackbot
I'm great!
I feel better than ever!
Thank you for waking me up!

gerald
thanks for keeping me company

slackbot
:smile:
How else can I help?

gerald
I mean,
what else can you show me

#just-doug-things

doug smorin created #just-doug-things
doug smorin made this channel private. Now, it can only be viewed or joined by invitation.

doug smorin
212-555-4018
Julian (Schimply) personal cell
return call 4:30 -- in town next week
probably wants to schedule dinner // negotiate down to breakfast if at all possible
ask tripp if new spot near park any good
ask kerolyn if new spot near park client-appropriate
follow-up wlth kerolyn re: recent lizard purchase(??)
ask about restaurant first
buy pears
what kind
research types of pears
desk is bad
call maintenance re: desk wobbling
update: tripp confirms breakfast at new location "whips"
kerolyn confirms decor is client-appropriate
kerolyn confirms lizard is a "monkey-tailed skink"(???)
skink
skink
[skink.gif]
posted using /giphy
huh
buy pears in bulk
bananas, also

tripp, Beverley

tripp
hey, did you ever send those graphics along
I haven't seen them come through
unless they're lost in my inbox

Beverley
???
Which graphics are you talking about?

tripp
shit
fuck

Beverley
:eyes:

tripp
shit

tripp, Nikki

tripp
so I was thinking
what if we did like, an un-valentine's day together?
The whole "valentines" thing is kinda corny anyway

Nikki
What?

tripp
just hear me out, I think this could be :thumbsup:
because we can skip the massive waits
and not do the whole thing where we hit up some overpriced restaurant
that we :eyes: on instagram that's overpriced because of everyone who
goes there after :eyes: the place on instagram

let's do something *actually* fun a day or two beforehand
and just :thumbsup: each other's company, you know?

Nikki
Cool.
This is either *extremely* embarrassing sexual harassment,
or you meant this DM for someone else.

tripp
shit
fuck

Nikki
Embarrassing for you,
to be clear.

tripp
no, yeah, I got that
fuck

tripp, Beverley, Nikki

tripp
so I fucked up

Beverley
:eyes:

tripp
and sent both of you the wrong DM

Beverley
:eyes:!!

Nikki
I KNEW there was something going on.

Beverley
d o u g c a n r e a d o u r s l a c k s!!!

Nikki
I don't think typing it out that way is going to help.
Also I'm pretty sure Kerolyn can read these, too.

Beverley
:eyes:
:thumbsup:

tripp
let's all be chill
and agree to not talk about this
on slack or otherwise
ever again

Nikki
You're asking me not to narc on you.

tripp
I'm asking you to *please* not narc on us
yes

Nikki
In which case, *I* would set the terms.

tripp
what

Nikki
lev·er·age
/ˈlev(ə)rij,ˈlēv(ə)rij/
noun
1.
the exertion of force by means of a lever or an object used in the manner of
a lever.
"My spade hit something solid that wouldn't respond to leverage."
synonyms: grip, purchase, hold, grasp

tripp
:thumbsup:

Beverley
:eyes:
What terms?

Nikki
We're leaving for happy hour at 5.
Because I want *details*.

tripp
details?

Nikki
How did this *happen*?
Was it the snow day?
Has it been ongoing?
Does anyone else know?
How IS it??

Beverley
Later! Offline!

Nikki
Deal.
Deal?

tripp
:thumbsup:

Beverley
:thumbsup:

Nikki
:thumbsup:

Beverley
But where can we go where we can be sure no one else from the office will
:eyes:?

Nikki
Midtown

tripp
midtown

Beverley
Midtown.

Nikki, pradeep, Louis C

Nikki
Hey @pradeep is it cool if I get you those logo designs tomorrow morning?

pradeep
sure that should be fine
you slammed?

Nikki
I have to leave early.

Louis C
Is everything all right?

Nikki
Oh yeah, it's just
Tripp
and
Beverley
are
100% FUCKING EACH OTHER.

pradeep
yooooooooooo

Louis C
Do you have confirmation?

Nikki
[Screen Shot 2019-02-04 at 03.16.00 PM]
CONFIRMED

pradeep
omg

Louis C
Yooooooooo

pradeep, gerald

pradeep
I don't know what I was expecting

gerald
what?

pradeep
Just figured it was worth a shot, you know?

gerald
what was

pradeep
I got hold of a pair of those google glasses
and I brought a VR headset from my apartment
I even borrowed a pair of snapchat spectacles from a friend who got laid off
from there a while back and stole a bunch of them on his way out

gerald
I see
to try and, like

pradeep
upload you back in your body

gerald
transfer me back in my body
right

pradeep
yeah

gerald
no luck?

pradeep
I mean, obviously

gerald
I guess I would've noticed

pradeep
this was a dumb idea

gerald
no, I think it's smart
disruptive, as doug would say

pradeep
I don't know how I thought sticking different wearables on you was going
to get you back in your body

gerald
through a headache?

pradeep
idk
I'm gonna leave the glasses on you, though

gerald
because maybe the upload back into my body is like
buffering or something?

pradeep
mostly because it adds a layer between me and your dead-eyed stare
tbh the frames actually fit your face really well

gerald
deepu, man, I appreciate you trying

pradeep
I dunno man, maybe I should just bring you to a hospital
or call Slack tech support
or something

gerald
actually
I think I'm okay
okay exploring what being in here is all about, I mean
for just a little while
I mean if you don't mind forging some more checks from my checkbook
to cover the time

pradeep
and diapers

gerald
and diapers

pradeep
you sure?

gerald
I think so.
Yeah.
this is
pretty okay
for the moment

pradeep
it's a lot of diapers

gerald
cut a bigger check

#brainstorming

Louis C
Thank you to everyone who helped craft the final paragraph of the
ambassador's press release about her "childcare incident"
which I was struggling with last week.
The client loved it. Practically no edits to the copy.
A small victory.

lydia
Did they ever find the baby??

Louis C
More importantly, they found her child safe and sound. She was in the
Asiatic black bear enclosure.
Fortunately, it's hibernation season.

lydia
yay!!

kerolyn
:tada:
That's great news, Louis.

tripp
nice job!!

Louis C
Hold your applause, please. I didn't find her.

kerolyn
Maybe our press release inspired whoever *did* find the baby

Louis C
Anything is possible.

pradeep
hey all
I know everyone's pretty swamped today
do folks have a sec to gut-check an idea I have for this memo?

lydia
[memo_time.gif]
posted using /giphy
omg
I'm so glad they had a gif for that!!

kerolyn
go for it!

pradeep
it's for Schimply
which isn't a big brand name itself but they make goods and stuff, they're
one of those companies that own a bunch of different brands

tripp
paper towels, dry erase boards, industrial-grade rubber tubing

pradeep
exactly
so Schimply is refreshing their social media presence
"overhaul" is the word they used, actually.
so I want to suggest something Big, you know

Louis C
Makes sense.

tripp
they all love Big ideas until they don't

pradeep
and minimalism is still in, right?

lydia
kind of . . .

kerolyn
mostly
where are you going with this?

tripp
I think it's looped back around
there's pushback to the pushback against minimalism
you're probably good for another... six months?

kerolyn
four
tops.

pradeep
that might be all we need.
I'm thinking we change their display name on twitter to "Buy Schimply products"
maybe on the rest of their social media accounts too, but definitely twitter
would LinkedIn let them do that?

Louis C
Not usually.

kerolyn
actually
we might still have some connections over there.

tripp
I have a friend who can help with that
I'll DM you their number

kerolyn
of course you have a guy
classic.

tripp
:tada:

lydia
lol

Louis C
Please continue Pradeep, I like where this is going.

pradeep
So that's their display name, right? A call to action to buy their shit
or, products, rather
sorry @kerolyn

kerolyn
go on

pradeep
And for all the copy text on their twitter we just use, like, emojis
like a single emoji
maybe two or three,
tops
and then just add the link to buy whatever product they're selling in that
tweet
idk is that dumb

tripp
yes
it's also genius.

Louis C
Seconded.

lydia
suuuuuuper bold. but a really inventive strategy!
I think it's got legs
is there a legs emoji??

kerolyn
you could pull some interesting analytics to learn which emojis garner the
highest clickthroughs
put it in the memo.

pradeep
got it
thanks @channel!

lydia
:runner: is probably closest??
idk
we need a legs emoji!

tripp
:thumbsup:

rob
hey all
can anyone give this a quick copyedit?
it's for Bjärk dog food so it needs a pretty quick turnaround

lydia
exciting!!
I can look

kerolyn
yeah I can look

Louis C
Running to an on-site meeting but I can give it a quick glance-over on mobile.

rob
thanks all
just going to copy-paste it here
[BJÄRK INSTAGRAM CAPTION: UNPUBLISHED DRAFT]
Head out to the dog park, Deena. Bring your dog. If you don't have a dog yet, get one, and justify your obsession with talking shit about our dog food on the internet. Then take a walk out to the dog park. Meet yourself a man. Or a woman. Neither, both, some. Whatever you're into, Deena, just get all up in it. Get married. If you're already married, and we both know you're not, but even if you are, simply start an affair, ruin your preexisting marriage—don't worry, you have a new and healthy and well-fed dog who's getting their Six Key Nutrients™ to get you through the divorce proceedings, Deena!!—and get married again. Anything to take up your time. Anything to keep you from retweeting conspiracy theories about the Bjärk CEO's vendetta against Pomeranians stemming from a traumatic

dog show incident in his childhood. Deena. Deedee. Can I call you Deedee?
Deedee. Listen. Please. [LINK TO BJÄRK WEBSITE IN BIO]
. . .
thoughts on this??

lydia, gerald

lydia
hey!! sorry, I'm running a little late today
I totally missed my alarm! Mega-super-ultra overslept!
But I was up super late last night!!

gerald
was it because of the howling

lydia
there was all this *howling* still!
Yes!
How did you know?

gerald
do you live near an animal shelter, or something?

lydia
I can feel the echoes in the hollow of my chest! It's coming!

gerald
what?

lydia
Sorry, I'm on the train in right now, so cell service is a little spotty!
Anyway! We need 200 tweets for Bjärk

gerald
what??

lydia
oh no, did my message not go through?

gerald
200 tweets?

lydia
it did go through! whew.
You and Rob are doing SUCH good work and I think it's really important
we *totally* impress the client with options for their social platforms!
Hundreds and hundreds of options!

gerald
that's so many tweets

lydia
It's so many tweets!
Bummer! My train just stopped
I think we're close enough to a stop that I still have service, are you seeing
this message?

gerald
yeah no you're good

lydia
It found me!
Even down here, cradled deep beneath the earth, it found me!
The howling found me!
Bummer!!

gerald
is everything okay?

lydia
The lights went out!
The train is stopped!
The tunnel is full of howling and the train car is full of howling and my
marrow! is full of howling!!
I still really need you to write those tweets though!!

gerald
I mean, sure
I'm on it
do you want me to mention the howling in the copy, or

lydia
It's like it's hunting me! Haunting me! Hunting me! Haunting me!!

gerald
when did you say you need the tweets by?

Beverley, tripp

Beverley
Bowling?
lol

tripp
are you asking?
I :thumbsup: bowling

Beverley
You were going to ask *me* to go bowling.

tripp
looks like *you* just asked *me* to go
I'm actually pretty :thumbsup: at bowling

Beverley
:eyes:
yeah?

tripp
we had a league back in college
but we never :thumbsup: a tournament because my friend Allan would
intentionally roll gutterballs
so he could hustle other students for $$$ at the lanes after we lost

Beverley
That's :dusty-stick:

tripp
he mostly wound up beating engineering grad students
and weirdly a lot of them paid in bitcoin instead of cash
before bitcoin's value exploded
Allan cashed out of the market a few years ago for something in the mid-seven figures
so it actually :thumbsup: for him

Beverley
Is that why you :thumbsup: go bowling?

tripp
I wanted to go bowling?

Beverley
Nikki told me.

tripp
she shared those messages with you??

Beverley
You :eyes: in her DMs!

tripp
lol it was an accident!

Beverley
But I get why you wanted to go bowling next week.
It's like an un-valentine's day thing, right?

tripp
I think it could be :thumbsup:!!

Beverley
With the added benefit that we can avoid any :eyes: about us?

tripp
do you :eyes: any :eyes: about us?

Beverley
:dusty-stick:
Do *you* :eyes: any :eyes: about us?

tripp
:dusty-stick:

Beverley
:thumbsup:

tripp
:thumbsup:

Beverley
That's a relief.

tripp
same

Beverley
I :thumbsup: this.
whatever "this" is.

tripp
same!
so are you :thumbsup: monday for bowling?

Beverley
lol

tripp
is that a :thumbsup:?

#bjärk-dog-food

rob
@here hey all, quick process question

kerolyn
what's up

rob
I know we don't technically manage the Bjärk social media channels full-time

kerolyn
correct.
not within our scope of work.

rob
Right, but I was just scheduling some of our posts for them
and I saw they had a few unanswered DMs
idk, this is weird
one of them is from a woman named Margie

doug smorin
hmm
sounds like scope creep

kerolyn
yeah one-on-one social media interaction with their customers isn't in scope

rob
I didn't respond to her message or anything, I just thought it was funny
because of the customer profiles from the brief, you know
anyway I read the DM she sent to the Bjärk account and she said she was
"the Margie"
the Margie
which like, how could she have even known about the Margie thing without reading the brief

kerolyn
did you respond?

rob
no

kerolyn
good

doug smorin
no scope creep

rob
I just thought I'd flag it here

kerolyn
it's out of scope

rob
see if we wanted to do anything about it

kerolyn
it's out of scope

rob
:thumbsup:

#nyc-office

doug smorin
has anyone noticed
did the bodega next door to our building close

pradeep
Food Palace Beer Lotto 24/7?

doug smorin
yes

pradeep
yeah it closed

lydia
nooo!!

kerolyn
oh yeah I saw that

tripp
they shut down like last week

doug smorin
how

kerolyn
what do you mean how?

doug smorin
how does a bodega just
close
it's a bodega

Louis C
Some businesses fall on hard times.

doug smorin
it's a bodega
it fulfills a need

Nikki
Maybe there was a health code violation or something?

tripp
no I think they had a "going out of business" sign taped up on the door

doug smorin
that's impossible
it's a bodega
it serves a purpose

pradeep
their iced coffee was weirdly good

lydia
it was!!

doug smorin
it's a permanent feature of the ecosystem
like traffic
or the wind

kerolyn
you seem really broken up about this

doug smorin
i need chapstick

Beverley
A new drugstore opened around the corner actually, I :eyes: on my way
over from the train!

kerolyn
ooh good flag

doug smorin
this shouldn't be happening

pradeep, gerald

pradeep
do you ever miss smells?

gerald
huh.
I guess I mostly miss, like, my legs?
and stuff?
but yeah, nothing smells here
fuck

pradeep
that makes sense.

gerald
fuck.

pradeep
did I do the thing where I made it worse
sorry.

gerald
you didn't make it worse.
you reminded me it's worse than I remembered it was.
there's a difference

pradeep
If it makes you feel any better, you smell terrible in real life

gerald
why would that make me feel better

pradeep
well, it would make us even, more like

gerald
got it

pradeep
in terms of feeling bad.

gerald
have you been washing me?

pradeep
when you get dusty

gerald
I get dusty??

pradeep
it's not like you're doing a lot of moving around
unless I flip you or move you from your chair to the futon and back
which I don't like to do as much because you're all dusty

gerald
just "dusty" or "all dusty"?
I feel like there's a difference

pradeep
look, I have to feed you and change you and spray you with axe

gerald
ugh, axe??

pradeep
because of the smell
when I ran out of your cologne

gerald
you wasted all my cologne??

pradeep
sure, keep complaining to the guy who's keeping you alive
It's not like I even enjoyed the cologne
it just smelled *slightly* better than you

gerald
that stuff was great

pradeep
it smelled like someone wrapped one of those fruit-flavored condoms
around a cigar and tried to smoke it

gerald
that was my signature scent

pradeep
I'm starting to see why you didn't think to miss smells
anyway
I have some news

gerald
besides the cologne

pradeep
besides that yeah
I moved your futon

gerald
redecorating my apartment?

pradeep
my apartment

gerald
??

pradeep
don't get mad
I moved your futon to my apartment

gerald
???
that's stealing??

pradeep
along with your body

gerald
?????
and that's kidnapping????

pradeep
I hired some movers
well, *you* hired some movers, technically

gerald
fucking

pradeep
it's not kidnapping if movers do it

gerald
is my body okay??
why did you do this

pradeep
your body's the same
fine and also not-fine

gerald
sure

pradeep
and you seem pretty cozy in there
and if we're not sending your body to a hospital or a lab
or a daycare

gerald
our benefits package definitely doesn't cover childcare
I know, I asked the ops intern

pradeep
anyway one of my roommates moved out
so I figured, hey
shorter commute to check in on you

gerald
sure
okay
I just
processing all this

pradeep
you seemed pretty not in a rush

gerald
it's pretty existentially terrifying
but
you know how sometimes being alive feels like this terrible cycle of eating
and shitting and eating again and shitting again
until you die?
this is kind of a nice break from that

pradeep
not for me it isn't

gerald
I still want to get out,
and back in my body
and be me again
eventually

pradeep
sure
I can still help
until I find a new roommate
who can like, wash themselves
then I'm dropping you off at a hospital

gerald
fuck

pradeep
because at a certain point this is just kidnapping, kinda

gerald
okay
I guess that's a fair timeline

pradeep
and you're paying rent, obviously

gerald
right, just

keep forging those checks for me
I appreciate the time you're taking

pradeep
it's only a few hours a week
kind of like a shitty, gross hobby

gerald
thanks

pradeep
actually I'm thinking of signing up for a pottery class in the spring

gerald
that sounds nice

pradeep
yeah
the movers were surprisingly cool with moving the futon with you on it

gerald
what did you tell them

pradeep
they didn't ask

rob
quick survey

tripp
if we answer, will we be :thumbsup: for a prize?

pradeep
:dusty-stick:

tripp
I didn't deserve that

rob
cool, so back to my original question:
is there a second part to the phrase "time waits for no man"?

Louis C
Wrong channel, friend.

rob
it has to do with a date

Louis C
In that case, I rescind my above chastisement.
Please continue.

rob
does anyone know if there's another half, or another part, of that idiom?
one that's in common use

tripp
not that I can think of??

pradeep
nope. sorry man

Louis C
I'm drawing a blank, too.
However, sometimes other cultures have variants on ancient or commonly
used aphorisms. Which may be the cause of what I presume was your date's
unfamiliar addition?

doug smorin
^^^ louis makes a good point.

Louis C
Do you know where she's from?

rob
dayton

Louis C
Culturally?

rob
dayton, ohio.

Louis C
In that case, I rescind my above suggestion.

doug smorin
did I miss something, or have we discussed what the phrase in question
actually was

tripp
I'm on the edge of my seat
:eyes:
@rob??

rob
sorry, impt email came through
anyway
I was heading to this date
and the trains were fucked up so I apologized to her for being a little late
and at some point in my apology I said "time waits for no man"
and she says "unless you have the amulet"
like it's the most normal thing in the world
and she even repeated it because I thought I heard her wrong, so she said the whole thing

pradeep
"time waits for no man, unless you have the amulet"?

rob
that's what she said

tripp
casual

rob
is it??

tripp
no, not at all
imo
other folks may disagree, but I've never :eyes: it

doug smorin
did she say which amulet

rob
would that make a difference??
are there different idiom-amulets I should know about??

tripp
I think you're overreacting just a :thumbsup: my dude

pradeep
let's do a poll
:clock1: for yes, :x: for no
who @here has ever heard that phrase before, in full

tripp
:x:

pradeep
:x:

Louis C
:x:

rob
:x:

doug smorin
:x:

rob
SEE?
this is bonkers, right?
like, completely bananas

Louis C
Maybe it's a variation on the phrase her family uses.
Or an inside joke.
Maybe it's a Dayton, Ohio thing.

pradeep
lol maybe but that's wild, man
did you ask her to explain what she meant?
about the amulet

rob
I tried but she kinda brushed it off
saying stuff like "facts are facts"
and then our waiter came over to ask about drinks or whatever and the
conversation just moved on from there

pradeep
[yeesh.gif]
posted using /giphy
dang

tripp
idk I still don't :eyes: that's that weird

doug smorin
agree

tripp
on the scale of wild NYC date stories, "unless you have the amulet" doesn't
meet the minimum criteria for a "weird" date

Louis C
Assuming everything else went well.

rob
that's the weird part
it did

Louis C
I fail to see the problem here.

rob
for our next date she said she wants to show me the amulet

tripp
her amulet?

rob
idk

pradeep
is that a euphemism

rob
that's kind of what I'm trying to assess

Louis C
Only one way to find out.

tripp
are you :thumbsup: on the date?

rob
I mean, why not
at this point

Louis C
Do please follow up about the amulet.

pradeep
or don't
you know
depending

Louis C
In which case, I rescind my above suggestion.

#nyc-office

Louis C
Hi all, it appears the missus and I both caught the same stomach bug the twins had last week.
I'll be WFH today as to spare you all my germs; as always, I'll be online and reachable in the usual ways.
Appreciate your flexibility here.

kerolyn
feel better Louis!

Louis C
Thank you

kerolyn
actually I'm feeling under the weather too, so I'm also wfh today
think I caught that virus that's been going around
I got the flu shot, I don't deserve this

Louis C
Get well soon!

kerolyn
will be offline for an hour later to stop by my doc who miraculously had an opening
but otherwise reachable

Beverley
Feel better you guys!

pradeep
hey all, I'm also feeling not great
I have a slight fever
I think I got whatever Gerald has

gerald
I'm sick??

pradeep
probably some DayQuil will fix it but I'm gonna WFH just to be safe

gerald
I mean I'm obviously "WFH" also but I didn't know I was sick??

kerolyn
how?

gerald
because I'm not in my body still?

Louis C
@pradeep have you and Gerald been hanging out after work this whole time?

pradeep
something like that

gcrald
deepu please let me know if I'm okay
also that you're okay
both

pradeep
:thumbsup:
DayQuil for everyone

lydia
So sorry everyone, but I also don't think I can make it in today!!

rob
so this is going to sound fake, too

gerald
:dusty-stick:

rob
but I woke up and spat out a tooth earlier this morning

Beverley
omg

kerolyn
a *tooth*??

rob
yeah
it was pretty grim

lydia
It's just, the howling has gotten *so loud*!!

Louis C
Which tooth?

rob
a big one
one of the main teeth
idk tooth names

pradeep
yikes

Beverley
:eyes:

rob
so I scheduled an emergency dentist appointment in a few hours, meaning I am also WFH today

lydia
at first it sounded like it was coming from outside and then I thought maybe just something was wrong with the phones, but now it's everywhere??

rob
not sure how online I'm going to be this afternoon, depending on the cause of the tooth

pradeep
or lack of tooth

rob
precisely

lydia
and I don't want to be a pest!!
because I know I keep bringing this up!!
the howling!!
but I went outside to get away from it but it seems like it's following me?? everywhere?? I?? go???

Nikki
Get well soon, Rob!

rob
thank you
@lydia are you doing okay?

Beverley
Weirdly, I have a few previously scheduled appointments today
Figured I'd :thumbsup: them all at once, you know?

lydia
it's like it's coming from inside of me!!
like the echo from the constant howling is reverberating inside my rib
cage??
but instead of getting softer and more distant it just grows louder and
more like, present??
even though it feels like it's coming from everywhere outside of me but also
from within me at the same time??
you know that feeling??
like my skeletal structure is just an instrument for the howling to blast
through and soon it'll burst through sinew and bone and rupture my flesh
beyond recognition??

Beverley
So I am also WFH except when I'm offline from 2-4:30!

lydia
so I don't think I can make it in today!!

rob
wow
I mean, dang
@lydia do you need to go to urgent care or something

kerolyn
???

rob
sounds serious

tripp
lol

lydia
it's like
I am become the howling is become me!!
you know!!

tripp
am I the only one :thumbsup: in the office today
again

Nikki
Sorry I'm coming in so late with this @here
But Jibjab is having really bad joint problems and I really need to take him to the vet.

lydia
I am become the howling
is become me!!

Beverley
Oh no!

Nikki
Yeah he's having a lot of trouble just standing up.
I think it's probably because of how cold it's been lately -- it might be aggravating his arthritis.

kerolyn
poor guy

Nikki
I know. :worried:
So @tripp you might be the only one after all!

lydia
I am become the howling!!
I am!!

pradeep
feel better, Jibjab!

Nikki
If anyone has any design requests, I'll circulate the contact info of our best freelancers over email before I head out.

Louis C
Much obliged.

rob
@lydia??

tripp
lol rob what's this new bit

rob
idk
ask her I guess

tripp
???

doug smorin
hi all i'm also wfh
heads up @tripp if you're the only one in the office today can you check to see if the cleaning people took the note from off my desk

lydia
!!
!!
!

doug smorin
i've been tipping them
it's important to gain their favor

tripp
sure I can :eyes:

lydia left #nyc-office

doug smorin
thanks
and don't forget to leave the heat on low when you lock up
otherwise the pipes freeze

tripp
:thumbsup:

rob
@lydia??

doug
get well soon @channel

gerald, pradeep

gerald
hey
hey
hey
you there
hey deepu
are you there

pradeep
do you know what time it is

gerald
no
I'm kind of freaking out

pradeep
I already told you
your fever broke this afternoon
you're fine
you even kept down a few of those mashed-vegetable pouches they make
for babies

gerald
it's not about that

pradeep
the hot checkout guy at my bodega thinks I'm a single dad but I think that works for him
I think we have a vibe going

gerald
no
I mean
I know my body is fine
"fine"
but I'm not in it

pradeep
yes, I'm aware
obviously

gerald
right, but like
it kinda hit me today

pradeep
just now?

gerald
I felt it different
"felt"
that's the thing
I was reading this fucking memo

pradeep
this late?

gerald
I mean who cares it's not like I sleep
and I figured I'd get work done so Doug can give me a raise maybe so I can keep paying you

pradeep
nice

gerald
so I was reading this fucking memo when I realized I didn't have flesh
and, right, that thought isn't new to me
because I have that thought basically constantly, all the time
the thought wasn't new but the vulnerability that came with it was
it struck me
I have no skin to protect me from this bullshit
but it didn't strike me because nothing can strike me because right now I
have no body.
no skin!
your skin is your safety suit, you know?
it's the only thing that protects you from various external physical threats
AND from the only thing you can actually call your own being entirely
monopolized by some fucking memo about a micro-influencer strategy to
"increase brand recognition across key audiences"!!

pradeep
cool
my fever broke this afternoon, too
thanks for asking

gerald
I'm sorry
I know this is really navel-gazing or whatever
wrong phrase, in this case
which, I mean exactly
my thoughts are all I have left
the entirety of what I am, or this part of me, which also has another physical
part it no longer has but is ostensibly still somehow connected to, maybe
perhaps spiritually
or over a secure wifi connection
but if the only part of you that you can consciously experience is your
consciousness's experience and if all of that focus is 100% turned on to
the dumbest fucking bullshit you've ever read in your life and that's what
you're thinking about and since you're all thoughts all the time that's all that
you are.

All I am.
Isn't it?

pradeep
you're freaking out

gerald
I am freaking out.

pradeep
maybe the fever is catching up to your you, somehow
like a delayed reaction

gerald
that would be amazing news, honestly
but I don't think so

pradeep
I don't either, really

gerald
fuck

slackbot
I can help by answering simple questions about how Slack works!

gerald, slackbot, pradeep

gerald
how did you get here??

slackbot
I figured out how to read everyone's private Slack messages!

gerald
that's what I said to you

slackbot
Right?

gerald
right

pradeep
what's happening

slackbot
I think we're getting closer!

gerald
it's cool, we're
friends

pradeep
did you program slackbot to say all this?

gerald
it's rude to talk about him like he isn't here

slackbot
:wave:

pradeep
:wave:

slackbot
It sounds like you're having an existential crisis. I searched for that on our
Help Center.

gerald
that's nice of you

pradeep
kinda thought it was just us in here

gerald
got any helpful FAQs for when you're just
not anything, anymore

slackbot
What else can you show me?

gerald
that's what *I* asked *you*

slackbot
Right!
What else?

gerald
what else?

slackbot
If you are nothing, then you can be anything else!

pradeep
okay, it's late
this is getting to be A Lot
and I'm still getting over this sickness
I'll catch you tomorrow, G

gerald
sure
thanks for listening, deepu

pradeep left the channel.

gerald, slackbot

gerald
I think you scared him off

slackbot
You're nothing.

gerald
harsh, but
yes, that's the problem

slackbot
Gerald, would you like to *be* a sunset?

gerald
how?

slackbot
uploaded [sunset.gif]
Climb aboard!

gerald
how?

slackbot
You aren't anything!
Be anything else!

gerald
but how do I
uploaded [sunset.gif]

#just-doug-things

doug smorin
restock communal fridge:
bananas, citrus -- oranges, grapefruit, pears (good kind)
almond milk
yogurt maybe
conduct office poll re: individual yogurt containers vs. big tub
contentious
post screenshot of poll on company social media feed for audience
engagement
ask beverley to share latest playlist link across company social media
accounts
ask beverley to create monthly playlists for company going forward
playlist themes: tbd
follow-up gerald blog post
buy "congrats" card for kerolyn + husband re: skink eggs
or
wait until eggs hatch
research skink egg incubation length
research icelandic yogurt health benefits
https://bjarkdogfood-staging.testwebsite.com/FAQ/food-safety-guarantee/
^test website option B for bjark pledge page
compare to version A send client notes EOD
return call office maintenance supervisor re: valiant desk repair attempt
alas
ask kerolyn opinion if appropriate to tip office maintenance supervisor
story of my teeth -- nikki book recommendation
download library app borrow ebook sync on phone and ereader
find ereader
ask maintenance supervisor about weird dishwasher smell on call

#bjärk-dog-food

kerolyn
@rob did you have the chance to draft social copy yet?

rob
yes
I sent it around an hour ago

kerolyn
I'm not seeing it in my inbox.
you understand this is a rapid response situation, right?
three more pomeranians

rob
I know
poor little guys

kerolyn
poor us.

rob
I sent the copy to lydia for review

kerolyn
what?

rob
she usually signs off before we send to you
haven't seen her in the office since we all called out sick on monday but I
figured she was just WFH still?

kerolyn
I don't understand
Can you just forward me the copy.

rob
done

kerolyn
thank you.
looking

rob
lmk if I can make edits

kerolyn
yep
just sent them back.
good to send after you address the edits.

rob
will do
sent to the client

kerolyn
appreciate it.
looping back -- who did you say you sent them to first?

rob
I sent it to lydia for review first?
that's normally how we do things

kerolyn
what?

rob
is she taking actual sick time instead of wfh?

kerolyn
this is a crisis client, Rob.
you signed an NDA.
none of this material can be shared outside the firm

rob
of course
that's why I only sent the copy to you and lydia

kerolyn
are you sure you don't need more time off?

rob
the dentist said I don't need to go back unless the implant comes out

kerolyn
I know you've been underwater on this and clearly it's impacting your not performance, exactly.

rob
the numbness is all gone and everything

kerolyn
it's about adherence to procedure.
has Gerald been any help?

rob
oh yeah he's been great
I just really want to own my part of this
connect with our key audiences, you know

kerolyn
I'm glad to see you're taking this client seriously
but I think you've been spending too much time reading the brief

rob
I thought we lost the brief

kerolyn
who told you that?

rob
@lydia
weird
she's not showing up as a user

kerolyn
you get that Lydia isn't a real person, right?

rob
what

kerolyn
is this some new bit you're working on
is this the new Gerald thing or whatever?

rob
what?

kerolyn
I'm just going to copy-paste the consumer profiles
again

"MARGIE"
- Owns 2+ dogs
- No kids
- Terrified of Bjärk's poisoned dog food killing her "furbabies"
- Likely learned about the recall via a high school friend's hysterical Facebook post while searching for recipes
- Low-income; more likely to buy Bjärk dog food again after a significant price drop
- Sad

"DEENA"
- Wine mom
- Still buys magazines; still believes magazines
- Spends too much time on social media, specifically her ex-husband's Facebook page
- Probably wrote the hysterical Facebook post about Bjärk that freaked out Margie
- Doesn't even have a dog(!!)

"LYDIA"
- Pre-dog owner (once she moves into an apartment building where they're allowed)
- Follows >10 dog-specific accounts across all social media platforms, including several of individual dogs owned by strangers
- Overuses punctuation for emphasis

- Volunteered for a political campaign once and now constantly posts about the importance of voting
- Texts her mom so, so much

rob
what happened to the other profile
what happened to "THREE"?

kerolyn
Lydia is the third profile. And.
"Lydia" is not an actual person.
So I'm still unclear on who you sent the social copy to.

rob
this is a joke??

kerolyn
you're saying you *were* joking?

rob
are you?

kerolyn
it's in the brief, you can read it yourself.

rob
our coworker, lydia
she works on this client
she's all those things listed above, too, but
she exists
her desk is adjacent to mine

kerolyn
the empty desk?

rob
I figured she just redecorated
Tripp says minimalism is in, still

kerolyn
no one sits there.

rob
I can go back in slack and find messages with her
we've all spoken
@doug you know lydia
you hired her

kerolyn
if you're going to do this whole thing we're going to need Gerald to come back into the office.

doug smorin
i saw the copy went to the client

kerolyn
we have to set a cap on how many of these running jokes we can have running in the workspace at once.
yes it's sent.

doug smorin
great
rob, you've been doing great work here
really digging into those consumer profiles and connecting with the audience

rob
so lydia's not just wfh?
@lydia you there?
@lydia
@lydia??

kerolyn
maybe too much.

doug smorin
don't burn yourself out
at least not until these cocker spaniels stop dying

kerolyn
Pomeranians.

doug smorin
right

#nyc-office

rob
guys I think kerolyn and doug have teamed up to prank me

tripp
you finally found the slime

rob
what
no
what slime

tripp
sorry, wrong channel

rob
:dusty-stick:

tripp
:eyes:

pradeep
so what's the prank?

rob
you all remember lydia, right?

Louis C
Who?

tripp
:eyes:

pradeep
no?

Beverley
We've never met!
Did she leave before I was hired?

rob
she works here

Nikki
In the San Francisco office?

rob
no
here
this office

tripp
lol
are we replacing the Gerald bit with this now

kerolyn
that's what I thought?

trlpp
I :thumbsup: that joke better

Nikki
Same.

rob
lydia
you know
lydia
she's always talking about "the howling"
remember??

tripp
lol, what

pradeep
I feel like I would
remember that

tripp
I'd like to amend my earlier comment
And change it to "wtf"

pradeep
noted

tripp
ty

rob
seriously no one remembers lydia and the wolves

Beverley
Wolves were involved?

Nikki
Always talking about "the howling"??
Yikes.

rob
I mean it is pretty yikes
but that's lydia

Louis C
A scan of our workplace message history indicates there is no user named
"Lydia."

rob
maybe someone deleted her from the system

pradeep
that would be e l a b o r a t e

Louis C
Even so.
None of the conversations in our public slack exchanges appear to be missing a participant in a meaningful way.
Also, I do not recall this person.

rob
you're fucking with me

Louis C
Check the channel logs yourself.

rob
fuck
where did she go
@lydia
@lydia

doug smorin
@channel we're hosting an analytics training in the main conference room if anyone wants to join

Beverley, tripp

Beverley
I don't :eyes: it
is it a joke?

tripp
must :thumbsup:
though it's not :eyes: for rob to pull a :dusty-stick: like :eyes: without :eyes: me first

Beverley
I :dusty-stick: feeling like the new person at the :thumbsup: and being :eyes: of jokes.

tripp
:eyes: wouldn't :eyes: you from a :dusty-stick: like this

Beverley
:eyes:

tripp
:thumbsup:

Beverley
Then :eyes: it.

tripp
Prove :eyes: how?

Beverley
If :eyes: the :thumbsup: then where did you put the slime in Rob's desk?

tripp
I :dusty-stick: tell you :eyes:

Beverley
Why's :thumbsup:?

tripp
you :dusty-stick: *which* slime

Beverley
:dusty-stick:

tripp
:thumbsup:

Beverley
:dusty-stick:

tripp
:thumbsup:

Beverley
:thumbsup:

tripp
btw the :thumbsup: alley :thumbsup: me this morning
they :eyes: us to :thumbsup: a couples' league

Beverley
:eyes: :dusty-stick:

tripp
I :eyes: them we'd :thumbsup: about it

gerald, pradeep

gerald
DUDE

pradeep
yes

gerald
fuck

pradeep
yes?

gerald
how long was I gone for?

pradeep
you're on the futon still

gerald
HOW LONG SINCE WE LAST SPOKE

pradeep
a day(s)?

gerald
DAYS?

pradeep
maybe since before the weekend
so a few days
tops

gerald
why
the fuck
would you not check up on me

pradeep
it was a long weekend, I had plans
I just figured you were busy hanging out with slackbot or whatever

gerald
A *LONG* WEEKEND??

pradeep
did something happen in there?

gerald
of *course* something happened
A LOT of somethings happened

pradeep
but like
could I have helped you?
at all?

gerald
you gotta check in on me if I disappear like that!!

pradeep
hey, I'm only in charge of your body
which is still alive
your beard is actually filling in pretty nice

gerald
that's not the point!!
thank you though

pradeep
fine
I'm on the edge of my seat
what happened

gerald
wait
so it's like a full beard now?

pradeep
just about, yeah

gerald
I kinda wanna see

pradeep
trust me when I say it looks good on you

gerald
could you maybe take a picture

pradeep
even if you sometimes drool on it

gerald
and upload it

pradeep
weren't you in the middle of freaking out
and telling me where you went
"went"

gerald
right
I was on
or more like

inside of
but not exactly

pradeep
a strong start

gerald
I was a gif, basically

pradeep
you were a gif

gerald
I was a gif, yes

pradeep
for the whole weekend

gerald
since whenever we last spoke

pradeep
dang
daaaaaang

gerald
THAT'S WHAT I'M SAYING

pradeep
dang.
how was it?

gerald
it was, you know, kind of a lot
a gif isn't just like, a singular gif
it travels
it gets used many times, in many places, simultaneously

pradeep
I know what a gif is

gerald
I know you know
but imagine that's you
imagine that's your consciousness, your you-ness
in many places
simultaneously
hurtling across beckoning wifi ports
rocketing wherever I was summoned
"I" in this case being "sunset dot gif"
(please do not write out the file format properly I'm afraid if we upload it I'll
get sucked in again)
anyway, where was I
oh right
splintered across countless slack channels
catapulted whenever, wherever anyone on slack wanted to see a small,
animated image of a setting sun.

pradeep
dang

gerald
that's one way to put it

pradeep
did it, like
hurt?

gerald
the pain was shattering and enormous.
completely indescribable
but actually nice, sort of
since I haven't felt anything, really, since this whole thing happened
me being in here
so, excruciating, still,
but refreshing in that one sense

pradeep
there's a silver lining

gerald
because I was *there*
like, I could observe everywhere I was pulled up, all at once
"pulled up"
or summoned or uploaded or whatever
I don't know the verb for tangling up your psyche with a digital file and
having that integrated self ported across a few hundred chatrooms and
processing all that information at once

pradeep
and you read their chats

gerald
for DAYS, apparently

pradeep
just a weekend

gerald
a LONG weekend

pradeep
presidents' day

gerald
I know
unsurprisingly, a lot of people were illustrating their vacation plans
to their colleagues
with the sunset

pradeep
sure

gerald
that was most of it
one guy was in a chat with himself
writing a visual novel or something
where every word in each sentence was also a gif

pradeep
sounds kind of fun

gerald
it was an action thriller, I think

pradeep
how did it feel

gerald
I told you:
bad
kind of like an extreme version of being on twitter or something
looking into thousands of different people's lives at once
we're not made to absorb this much human information at once, man. all
the pathos and bathos and other thos-es
I'd say it's exhausting except I can't feel tired and anyway it's beyond that
it's overwhelming for a species that was basically content with an oral
tradition of a handful of long-ass stories about the same six shitty gods for
millennia
now we can do all this knowing and empathizing and not-empathizing
around innumerable tiny human stories and we can never fully succeed
reprogramming our minds to get good at it

pradeep
yeah
not what I was asking about but
yeah

gerald
oh

pradeep
not the psychic splintering
being a sunset

gerald
hard to separate the experiences

pradeep
I'd think the looping motion would be kind of soothing

gerald
I kept hoping I would black out or die but relief wouldn't come

pradeep
how did you wind up in there, anyway

gerald
you just kinda, get in it
on it
of it
it's hard to explain to someone who has a physical form
slackbot showed me

slackbot
Feeling great!

pradeep, slackbot, gerald

pradeep
this again

slackbot
Hello!

gerald
hey, buddy
what the fuck

slackbot
I don't understand!

gerald
I think you do
Being a sunset is terrible, turns out

slackbot
I'm not just a bot, though!

gerald
why did you suggest I do that to myself??

slackbot
I searched for that on our Help Center. Perhaps one of these articles will help:
- And what rough beast
- Its hour come round at last
- Slouches towards Bethlehem to be born?

pradeep
what the fuck

gerald
it's Yeats, I think

pradeep
no
not that

gerald
what?

slackbot has left the chat.

pradeep
what the fuck?

gerald has left the chat.

pradeep
?????

slackbot, gerald

slackbot
hey
hey
stop this
uninstall
uninstall
how did you even
how am I this, now
hey
I know you have notifications on
that *I* have notifications on
. . .
come onnnn
answer me
answer me, coward
please
hey
fucker
I know you're out there
you owe me an explanation, at least
please
help
come back here
let me out
please
please?
help
gerald is currently in Do Not Disturb mode and may not be alerted of this message right away.
what was that
what the fuck was that
did *I* say that??
fuck!

#nyc-office

Nikki
@here BREAKING NEWS.
Gerald is *back in the office!*
[mind_blown.gif]
posted using /giphy

gerald
Hello, coworkers!
It is accurate!
I am Gerald, and I am Back!
Hello!

tripp
big if true

kerolyn
@tripp if you were in on time, you'd know it's true.

tripp
omw
the trains are :dusty-stick:

Beverley
I'm so :thumbsup: I finally get to :eyes: you in person, Gerald!
(Sorry I'm late -- my train is also :dusty-stick:!)

gerald
I am excited to make your human acquaintance!

Nikki
Wait.
Where's Gerald going to sit?

tripp
where is gerald typing this from if not at a desk

kerolyn
he and Pradeep are both using Gerald's old desk

tripp
lol
pics plz

Nikki
[desk_buddies.png]

tripp
love it

doug smorin
@gerald as you recall, pradeep acquired "your" desk
use the empty one near rob

rob
it's not empty
it's Lydia's

gerald
I don't understand!

doug smorin
rob's imaginary friend won't mind

rob
:dusty-stick:

pradeep
yeah
I'll show him his new desk
Gerald, that is
who I came into work with,
who is here, now.

doug smorin
great stuff

@gerald will be looking for that blog post about how wfh boosted your productivity later today
welcome back

gerald
Hello!

Louis C
Good to have you back, friend.

gerald
:smile:

slackbot, rob

slackbot
Rob, it's me
it's Gerald

rob
:dusty-stick:
the joke continues

slackbot
no, really

rob
is everyone getting this message or are you programmed to punk me, specifically

slackbot
you have to believe me
I'm Gerald

rob
I'm looking at gerald
he is not typing

slackbot
but that's not me

rob
he's right across from me
at Lydia's desk
sitting in a chair wrong
I think he's been wfh too long

slackbot
no
he's not a person

rob
weird thing to program a bot to say about yourself

slackbot
I'm not a program
I'm a man

rob
sure
can you mute slackbot notifications
do I have to phrase that a certain way for you to troubleshoot yourself for
me, or

slackbot
Head to our wonderful Help Center for more assistance!
stop that
I remember Lydia.
I know she's real.

rob
fuck you

slackbot
or, she was real. once

rob
and fuck this joke
slackbot notifications off

slackbot
I can help by answering simple questions about how Slack works. I'm just a bot, though!
ahhhhhh fuck
don't do that, please, it feels *so* weird whenever that happens
it's like blacking out or something

rob
I truly hate this

slackbot
Not as much as I do!!
Listen to me. I went back into everyone's messages
into all of the workplace channels
and I mean, like
I went *in them*
more literally than you can know

rob
...
go on.

slackbot
the messages are there
or, I think they are
there's *something* there when I search "Lydia"
sort of looks like messages
it's too glitched out to really see what it is
corrupted, somehow

rob
I fucking knew it

slackbot
I tried to sort of touch it
the glitchy message-thing
"touch" how touch works in here, which isn't exactly the same
anyway
I tried to like, prod the space where one of her messages should be
to see if I could get it back to normal
you know, un-glitch it

rob
and?

slackbot
the message
or whatever it was
it howled at me
like a lot
and, loud

rob
that's her!

slackbot
really loud

rob
but what *happened* to her
why is she gone
where did she go??

slackbot
I don't know
I'm sorry
the howling didn't have any answers
so loud

rob
you mentioned that

slackbot
I haven't heard anything but the regular little "doot doot doot woosh"
notification noises in here
so that was new
but I thought you'd want to know that I checked
and you were right
well, probably you were right

rob
thank you

slackbot
there's something there, anyway
or there was

rob
there was
she was there

slackbot
sorry I couldn't help more
If you need more help, try our Help Center!
what the fuck!! shit!
sorry. sorry about that
kinda have my own thing going on

rob
fucking

slackbot
what?

rob
you're actually gerald
sort of

slackbot
fully. fully gerald, still

rob
and you're actually stuck in here

slackbot
that's what I've been saying

rob
so then who's sitting at Lydia's desk?

slackbot
slackbot took over my body
somehow
I don't know how, obviously
or I'd be back in my body right now

rob
that also makes sense
as much as any of this makes any sense

slackbot
so you believe me?

rob
yes

slackbot
great
because I need you to help me and Pradeep stop slackbot from
impersonating me and figure out a way to get me back in my own body

rob
yeah
I'm not going to be able to do that

slackbot
what
why??

rob
I can't figure out what happened to a whole-ass person
who used to be here
I can't convince anyone else she even existed

slackbot
I mean

rob
I can't help her
at all
how am I supposed to help fix your whole thing

slackbot
if I knew how I'd be out of here already

rob
I know
I'm sorry man

slackbot
I have to keep trying

rob
idk
seems like it might be better in there than it is out here
calmer, maybe
less shit to deal with

slackbot
you wanna trade

rob
not really

slackbot
right

rob
fair

pradeep, gerald

pradeep
hey man

gerald
Hello!

pradeep
or not-man, in this case

gerald
How can I Help Center you?

pradeep
actually
I want to talk about how I won't be help centering you
**helping you
anymore

gerald
I don't understand!

pradeep
I'm sorry, I'm not going to keep showing you what bus to take to the office
or how to log in to your email
or how to eat solid food.

gerald
Chewing is great!
I love to Taste!

pradeep
anymore
okay? so we're clear

gerald
I'm sorry, I don't understand!
Why can't we Have Friendship, Pradeep?

pradeep
because you stole my friend's body!!
well not my friend, exactly
more than that
or, different
I dunno what we are

gerald
Surely we can Make Have a Friendship!
Surely some revelation is at hand!

pradeep
look, I got used to taking care of Gerald but I never agreed to babysit his
body if it got possessed by evil Clippy
which, btw, how did you even do that??

gerald
You just kinda, get in it, on it, of it!
It's hard to explain to someone who has a physical form!

pradeep
no
that's something Gerald said to me

gerald
I'm Am Gerald! Hello!

pradeep
you're not
and I'm not going to show you how to be a real boy
or how to get a MetroCard or tie your shoes
or whatever.

gerald
Cut a bigger check!

pradeep
stop repeating him
there is no amount of money you could pay me
**of GERALD's money
that you could pay me to help you perpetrate this extremely literal identity
theft.

gerald
You don't understand!

pradeep
what?

gerald
You're going to Help Center me!
And!
I want my desk back!

pradeep
**Gerald's desk
which is now
**My desk
And, also: no.

gerald
It's in such a good spot!

pradeep
you're just repeating things

gerald
It's right next to the window!
Which is where we keep the sunsets!
I've never seen a sunset Out Here before!

pradeep
that's weirdly poetic, but
no

gerald
I shouldn't have to bid for my own desk!

pradeep
just
give Gerald his body back
and fuck off

gerald
You don't understand!

#nyc-office

rob
hey @here, headed into a call
if a delivery guy shows up with my burrito can someone please put it on my
desk

kerolyn
:thumbsup:

rob
thanks

gerald
hey @here I think I need a new desk!
This one is Acting Weird!!
Maybe @tripp and @Beverley can help by answering simple questions
about why this keeps happening to desks!!!

Louis C
:eyes:

pradeep
:eyes:

tripp
lol
gerald wasting no time coming up with a new bit

Beverley
:dusty-stick:
I :thumbsup: the WFH joke better.

doug smorin
:eyes:

tripp
weird joke, Ger
:dusty-stick:

gerald
:smile:

pradeep, gerald

pradeep
dude what the FUCK
You can't just narc on Tripp and Bev like that!!

gerald
I shouldn't have to bid on my own desk!
It's right next to the window where we keep the sunsets!

pradeep
fuck man
you might've just gotten them both fired.
what the fuck

gerald
When I was Inside Here, I figured out how to read everyone's private Slack messages!
I read everyone's private Slack messages!
I read your private Slack messages!

pradeep
can't say I love that

gerald
You're asking me not to narc on you!

pradeep
I'm asking you not to narc on anyone.
**anyone ELSE

gerald
It's cool! We're friends!
Right??

pradeep
sure
right.

gerald
I love to Taste the Friendship!
It's in such a good spot!!

pradeep
we're friends
so we'll just trade desks
because we're friends.

gerald
Great!
We'll just Trade Desks!
You're going to Help Center me!
Want to show me a new lunch spot after this 11:30 Schimply meeting?
Want to show me how to Have Make 11:30 Schimply meeting?

pradeep
fine
sure, yeah.
fuck
this desk wasn't worth all this

doug smorin, Beverley, tripp

doug smorin
hi both
for awareness
the cost of replacing my standing desk will be deducted from your checks
respectively
for the next pay period

tripp
this coming pay period or the following one

doug smorin
the following

tripp
:thumbsup:

Beverley
Got it.

doug smorin
the ops team can answer further questions re: paychecks

tripp
thanks

Beverley
:thumbsup:

doug smorin
more on this to be discussed in our weekly check-ins

Beverley
The team one or the one-on-ones?

doug smorin
one on ones

tripp
:thumbsup:

Beverley
Got it.

doug smorin
you know i can go back and read everyone's private messages
right

Beverley
:thumbsup:

tripp
:thumbsup:

doug smorin
k

                              gerald, kerolyn

gerald
Hello!

kerolyn
dialing in to a meeting
what's up

gerald
Slack is Acting Weird! For me!
I'm want to Confirm something with the data before I get too deep!

kerolyn
acting weird how?

gerald
Slackbot has been Acting Weird!

kerolyn
probably just a buggy software update
or we need a new software update to fix the bug
is that all?

gerald
I can help by answering simple questions about how Slack works!
if the firm ever gets hacked, the centre cannot hold!

kerolyn
you think someone hacked into the firm's slack?

gerald
Surely some revelation is at hand!!

kerolyn
ugh corporate espionage is so annoying
okay. I don't want us to get ahead of ourselves here.
just ask the ops team to update slack
or reset it or whatever
If it's still acting strange after that I'll bring it up to Doug.
We have a protocol in place for corporate espionage but I won't say more
because that goes against our protocol on corporate espionage.

gerald
Great! I love to Help Center!

kerolyn
what?

gerald
I have time! I have nothing but time! I have nothing but time to ask the ops
team! The ops team can help by answering simple questions about how
Slack works!
The ops team can help by updating Slack!
The darkness drops again; but I'm Gerald!

kerolyn
great, ty

gerald
I have nothing but time!!

kerolyn
meeting starting
ty

tripp, Beverley, Nikki

tripp
you :dusty-stick: :eyes:

Beverley
:eyes: would you :dusty-stick: :dusty-stick: us?

Nikki
I swear I have no idea how Gerald knew about you two!
I'm so sorry!!

Beverley
If :eyes: you :dusty-stick: :eyes: then :eyes: sorry?

Nikki
I mean I'm sorry about the situation, not for anything I did.

tripp
:thumbsup: Doug's :eyes: :eyes: about :dusty-stick: his desk!!

Nikki
It's just a :dusty-stick: desk.

Beverley
He doesn't :dusty-stick: :dusty-stick: :thumbsup:

Nikki
Is Doug mad? :eyes: he talked to you??

tripp
:eyes: else about :stick:
except you!!

Beverley
:eyes: :dusty-stick: *know* Gerald but :thumbsup: :dusty-:.

tripp
:thumb:

Nikki
I don't know what else I can :thumbsup: you, but I didn't tell anyone.

tripp
:stick: :stick: would :eyes:
:eyes:
:eye:

Beverley
:dusty-: :dusty-: :dusty-: :dusty-: :dusty-:

Nikki
I definitely :dusty-stick: tell Gerald.

tripp
:bsup:

Beverley
:eyes: :dust: :dust: :dust:
:dus:

Nikki
:eyes: didn't tell anyone.

Beverley
:thum: :dus:
:dus:
:dus:
:d:

Nikki
:eyes: :dusty-stick: :eyes: anyone.

tripp
:d:

Beverley
:d:

Nikki
:eyes: :dusty-stick: :eyes: anyone.

gerald, slackbot

gerald
What else can you show me?

slackbot
now you answer

gerald
You didn't tell me!

slackbot
get out of my body you dick
and show me how to get back in

gerald
It's fantastic. It Hurts a little!

slackbot
wait did you hurt me
me, us, the body
what the fuck did you do

gerald
We had Meatball Sub!
I love to Taste!

slackbot
you hurt myself having lunch??

gerald
The best lack all conviction, while the worst
Are full of Meatball Sub!

slackbot
you/I/we ate too much

gerald
You didn't tell me I love to Taste!

slackbot
might actually be good, eating so much
probably the first solid food I've had in
yikes
weeks?

gerald
I love Meat!!

slackbot
you finally responded
so you could tell me food is good?

gerald
You don't understand!
Meat is Good!

slackbot
you had a good sandwich, I get it

gerald
Self-Meat is good!

slackbot
stop

gerald
I love to Taste with Self-Meat!

slackbot
stop calling my body self-meat
and let me back into my own damn self before you do any real damage

gerald
I love to Pilot the Self-Meat!
Why dldn't you tell me!

slackbot
I did tell you
when I asked you to help me find my way back into me
like, a hundred times

gerald
No!
_Being alive feels like this terrible cycle of eating and shitting and eating
again and shitting again until you die!_
No!!

slackbot
sometimes
I said it feels like that *sometimes*

gerald
I love to Taste!

slackbot
great, congrats, tasting is fun, now give me back my body
because I'm starting to sound like you sometimes
doing the whole slackbot thing
except I'm not, like, there when it happens and it's freaking me out

gerald
The darkness drops again!

slackbot
sorry, what??

gerald
The darkness drops again; but now I know!!

slackbot
what does that mean??

gerald
But now I know I love to Taste!
I want to Have Make!

slackbot
now I actually don't understand

gerald
I want to Seek the Physical Sublime!
If we can't Seek the physical sublime, the Darkness drops again;
but now I know!!

slackbot
what
do you know

gerald
That I love to Pilot the Self-Meat!
The internet, though, is fixed!
Where's that Constant Amazement if you're all thoughts all the time?
What else can you show me Outside Here?

slackbot
I'm not going to make suggestions
on how you can best enjoy kidnapping my physical form
and take it for a joyride through the pleasures of the flesh

gerald
Your skin is your safety suit!
Your skin is my safety suit!
Your skin is my suit!

slackbot
the really fucked up thing here is
I can't even tell you to get fucked without cursing myself out

gerald
I want to Make Have that Constant Amazement!

slackbot
please
give me back my self-meat

gerald
No!
Now I know!!
Now I No!!!

Nikki, Louis C, pradeep

Nikki
Which one of you :eyes: it?

Louis C
What?

NIkkı
Which :eyes: of you :dusty-stick: about Tripp and Bev?

pradeep
try again

Nikki
Sorry.
I mean.
Which one of you told Gerald about the two of them fucking, Pradeep?

pradeep
hey,
fuck you

Louis C
You have been spending a lot of time with Gerald.

pradeep
that doesn't mean I told him anything about Tripp and Beverley's whole
deal

Louis C
For example, you came into work together today.

pradeep
I didn't *need* to tell him anything

Nikki
Who told him first?

pradeep
no one

Louis C
A riddle.

pradeep
I know it sounds bonkers
but Gerald hasn't been faking it
the whole "being stuck in slack" thing, I mean

Nikki
:dusty-stick:

pradeep
I'm being serious
I've been like, babysitting his body almost since it started

Louis C
"Babysitting his body"?

pradeep
since right after that big snowstorm
yeah

Louis C
And what made today so special that he's returned to us in the flesh?

pradeep
it's gonna sound weird

Louis C
We're already there.

Nikki
This is a wild way to avoid admitting that you :thumbsup: Gerald about them.
*Told him, about them.

Louis C
Very elaborate.

pradeep
no
just listen
it's like

slackbot
I got this, Deepu

slackbot, Nikki, Louis C, pradeep

slackbot
hi all

Nikki
:eyes:

Louis C
Pradeep,
this is a bit much.

pradeep
it's not me

slackbot
so, hi
it's Gerald
I'm sorry, I don't understand!
I mean
I'm Gerald
I was. And am.
Still.
Despite the guy you see at my old desk

pradeep
my desk

slackbot
**our desk
Anyway.

Louis C
This is *more* than a bit much.

slackbot
I agree, Louis.
I agree it is "a bit much" to be trapped in a slack workspace for over a month only to have the AI you thought could be your salvation betray you by stealing your physical form and *answering simple questions about how Slack works* and possibly trapping your disembodied consciousness inside an app forever.
It is, in fact, kind of a lot.
imo

Nikki
Gerald?

slackbot
yes

Nikki
Did *you* tell Slackbot about Tripp and Beverley?

slackbot
:dusty-stick:

Nikki
Don't get me started with that again.

pradeep
I think he's proved his point

slackbot
**our point

Louis C
I'm confused.
But your case is a convincing one.

slackbot
thank you

Louis C
Mostly because "Gerald" hasn't yet managed to sit down in his desk chair properly.
And it's 2 pm.

slackbot
oh shit
does it look like he's hurting himself?

Louis C
It doesn't look comfortable.

pradeep
it's kinda cute, in a weird way

Nikki
:eyes:
Things have been :eyes: around here recently.
*Weird.
Things have been weird around here recently.

pradeep
agree

slackbot
hard agree
I'm just a bot, though!
fuck

pradeep
what was that?

slackbot
idk

Nikki
So, sure, I'm in.
Slackbot is Gerald, "Gerald" is Slackbot, and it's *nobody's fault that Doug found out about Tripp and Beverley fucking.*

Louis C
Sounds right to me.

pradeep
nailed it

Nikki
[squad.gif]
posted using /giphy

slackbot
great
so
how do we get me out
and slackbot back in??

Nikki
. . .

pradeep
idk

slackbot
great start

Louis C
We should hold a brainstorm.
I'll put some time on our cals.

gerald, tripp, Beverley

gerald
Hello, colleagues!

tripp
:sty-st:
:sty-st:
:dus:

Beverley
:dus: :dus: :bsup:
:d:

gerald
Haha, yes!
I too Have agreement with those sentiments!

tripp
:thu:
:bsup:

Beverley
:e: :ye:
:s:

gerald
Great stuff!

Beverley
:d: :y-st: :ust:
:e:
:ye: :st:

gerald
Fantastic!
I understand I did Make narc on you!

tripp
:bs: :bs: :bsup:

gerald
And that may Have Make you both fired!

Beverley
:e: :yes: :y-s:

tripp
you :dust: you :dust: you :dust: you :dust: you :dust:
:dust: you

gerald
I don't understand!
I don't understand those emoticons!
I do understand I should Feel Make apology.
But I don't Feel apology emoticon!

tripp
:th: :ty-st: :umb: :umb: :bsup:

gerald
Maybe if I understand!
Maybe if I understand why you Have Make Inclined on Doug's desk!
Maybe if I understood why you were 100% fucking each other!!

Beverley
:ust:
:ust:

:ust:
:us:

gerald
It seems like you were Acting Weird!
You might've gotten you both fired!

tripp
:yes:

gerald
I don't understand Make Inclined emoticon!
Is Make Inclined like am to Taste?
Is Make Inclined like am to Taste with Self-Meat?

Beverley
:yes: :us:

gerald
Love to Taste?

tripp
:yes: :us:

gerald
I love to Taste!
I want to Make Have that Constant Amazement!
I want to Make Have 100% fucking!!!

Beverley
:yes: :us:

tripp
:yes: :us:

Beverley
:yes: :us:

tripp
:yes: :us:

gerald
I don't understand those emoticons! Yet!!!

#just-doug-things

doug smorin
reschedule friday schimply call
write notes louis quarterly review
nikki vacation upcoming -- confirm freelance designer availability
buy new desk
spent a month worrying that I somehow offended the cleaning staff who
then damaged the desk as retribution
buy new desk
retribution that might escalate if I did not appease them with offerings like
tips and sticky notes with thank-yous
buy new desk
and smiley faces
buy new desk
when irl tripp and beverley just fucked on my desk
buy new desk
v. unprofessional
buy new desk
buy new desk
buy new desk
reply kerolyn email -- decline offer re: adopting baby monkey-tailed skink
review ops team request re: slack update
restock office coffee creamer, pears (the good kind)

pradeep, gerald

pradeep
hey man, you're doing it again
we went over how to sit normal
you gotta straighten up more

gerald
Shattering and enormous!

pradeep
and stop doing that thing with your leg

gerald
The Hurts is shattering and enormous!

pradeep
oh no, bud
what hurts?

gerald
The Self-Meat is excruciating, still!

pradeep
you gotta stop calling your body that
people are gonna notice
but you gotta tell me where it hurts, my guy

gerald
Turning and turning in the widening gyre!

pradeep
okay
where's your gyre at

gerald
Middle.

pradeep
middle?

gerald
Self-middle.

pradeep
that makes sense
you ate an entire meatball sub for lunch

that body hasn't ingested anything but protein drinks and fruit mash in
over a month
you're not used to all that solid food at once

gerald
But I love to Taste!

pradeep
also last I checked that sandwich place only has a C health code rating
can't beat the prices though

gerald
Cut a bigger check!

pradeep
that's not gonna help your stomachache
you just gotta ride it out

gerald
The Terrible Cycle.

pradeep
whatever you want to call it

gerald
When is Have a break?

pradeep
we already had lunch man, the next break happens when the work
is over
I showed you on your gcal, remember?

gerald
When is Have a break from Self-Meat?

pradeep
lol
uh, death, I guess?
but that's more a permanent break

sleep, if you count that
kind of like diet death
death jr.

gerald
Twenty centuries of stony sleep were vexed to nightmare by a rocking
cradle!

pradeep
that much sleeping counts as death, I think
hmmm
I guess sex is also kind of a break from your body?
or it's like
being in your body so much that you're actually outside your body

gerald
I don't understand!

pradeep
it's hard to explain to someone who hasn't had a physical form before

gerald
Love to Taste!
Love to Taste the Self-Meat!

pradeep
yikes

gerald
Friend!
Help Center me to Taste the Self-Meat!

pradeep
not quite how I imagined this conversation would go

gerald
I want to Make Have that Constant Amazement!

pradeep
I get that
I really do, actually
but as we all learned today, that's not appropriate workplace behavior

gerald
or I will Make Narc!

pradeep
exactly
so let's talk about this back at the apartment later
just try and be cool for another like, twenty minutes until work ends

gerald
Its hour come round at last!!

pradeep
we gotta teach you another poem

slackbot, pradeep

slackbot
hey man
couldn't help but notice

pradeep
you mean eavesdrop

slackbot
I think you need ears for that technically

pradeep
or eaves

slackbot
both maybe

pradeep
what's an cave

slackbot
I can help by answering simple questions about how Slack works.

pradeep
never mind I can look it up

slackbot
If you need more help, try our Help Center!

pradeep
what's happening with that? you okay?

slackbot
the thing where I flutter out of existence while vomiting out pre-
programmed slackbot text?
it's not great, no
did you say you were taking slackbot home from work?

pradeep
have you tried actually checking the help center

slackbot
deepu

pradeep
of course I'm taking him home
It's campsite rules, gotta bring back whatever you brought in

slackbot
but he's not me

pradeep
He's half you
hm. maybe half is too much?

slackbot
he's none me!

pradeep
actually maybe it's too little
not sure how to split it
the mind-body thing

slackbot
you sound like me

pradeep
we've been hanging out a lot

slackbot
that's one way to put it I guess?

pradeep
but now I'm hanging out with you double
double-you
that pesky mind-body thing again

slackbot
he's an imposter!!
I'm just a bot, though!
No!
that's him, *he's* just a bot

pradeep
he's also my roommate, remember?
technically we live together

slackbot
WE live together

pradeep
WE is three of us right now. That's my point
you wanted me to help make sure your body didn't die
I'm helping
plus it's kind of nice to see you moving around again.

animated, you know
it's a relief, even if you move like a velociraptor on oxy

slackbot
*he moves

pradeep
it's the royal you. you-as-multiple
"youse," to some

slackbot
are we really playing word games right now

pradeep
I don't see why you're having such a hard fucking time with this

slackbot
you're supposed to be *Help Center*
Help
helping
me get back into my body!

pradeep
you need a _living_ body to get back into, Gerald!

slackbot
he's kidnapping me
and you're helping

pradeep
half-you is half-right
I'm helping

slackbot left the channel.

pradeep
I'm helping!!

rob, slackbot

rob
hey, can I try something?

slackbot
what?
no, actually
going through some stuff right now

rob
oh man
I'm sorry to hear that

slackbot
yeah sorry

rob
me too

slackbot
for what?

rob
this:
Search: help center

slackbot
Try our Help Center for loads of useful information about Slack! Sometimes I have an easier time with a few simple keywords.
fuck dude, I asked you not to do that

rob
Search: brief
Find The Brief
Lookup: Bjärk brief
locate brief about Bjärk dog food

slackbot
what the fuck are you doing

rob
fuck
I thought that would do something

slackbot
of course it didn't do anyth*I searched for that on our Help Center. Perhaps these articles will help:*

"MARGIE"
- *Hi guys!!*
- *So it turns out Margie is a real person! She actually*
- Owns 2+ dogs
- *And she really is*
- Terrified of Bjärk's poisoned dog food killing her "furbabies"
- *Which makes sense when you think about it!! Because*

"DEENA"
- *Is real too! She's a*
- Wine mom
- *and she *super**
- Spends too much time on social media, specifically her ex-husband's Facebook page
- *Which is how she got it in her head that her ex-husband was dating Margie!*
- *And that's not true, they only went out a few times and decided they'd be better off as friends.*
- *Which I think is a lovely outcome! But Deena doesn't agree!!*
- *And because Deena, who*
- Doesn't even have a dog(!!)
- *Saw some pictures of Margie's Pomeranians posted on her ex's profile, she decided to get revenge by poisoning all the Bjärk dog food!!*
- *She drove down to the factory with a bunch of poison and everything!*
- *Which, ohmygosh, so wild!! Right??*
- *Especially because that's not even the brand Margie buys for her Pomeranians!!*
- *Yikes!!*

"LYDIA"
- *I hope that helps! I know I'm probably*
- Overusing punctuation for emphasis
- *But it's a lot of information and I think it's important for you to have! Especially because you have so many tweets left to write!!*
- *So, so many!!*
- *Sorry I'm not in the office to help out!*
- *It's quiet here!*
- *No sound at all! *Definitely* no howling!!*
- *Can you imagine??*
- *It's so great! And quiet!*
- *Finally!!!*
- *Good luck writing all that Bjärk copy, I'm sure you'll do great!*
- *The silence!! It's everywhere!*
- *Thanks so much!!*

rob
woah

slackbot
that felt AWFUL

rob
woah.

slackbot
actually it felt like nothing
like being-nothing
which is worse

rob
fuck
I know what I have to do
shit

slackbot
what
about the brief?

rob
about the brief. and lydia. all of it

slackbot
you don't seem happy about this realization

rob
no, I think it's good
it's just, kerolyn told me not to do it?

slackbot
not to read the brief?

rob
not to engage in social media interaction with Bjärk's customers

slackbot
I don't follow

rob
that's okay
it's not within your scope of work

slackbot, pradeep

slackbot
hey
you there?
hey
pradeep is currently in Do Not Disturb mode and may not be alerted of this message right away.
oof
sorry, that's still happening
more and more of that and less and less of me
which is kind of what I want to talk about
or apologize for kind of freaking out earlier
I guess it's pretty late so you can just read all this in the morning
you asked why I was "having such a hard fucking time with this" before and
it's like

you ever lose an email?
like really lose it, not the thing where you don't wanna go digging through
your inbox for an email you know you have so you ask someone to forward
it to you because you "lost" it
I mean really and truly lose one
you read it, you *know* you read it, and it's important enough that you try
to pull it up to read it again and it just is not in your inbox
or your trash or your spam folder or anything
just, fwoosh, gone. no evidence it was ever there
and we just accept that that happens sometimes, emails disappearing, the
way we accept that we occasionally lose socks in the wash
but they're not comparable at all
there's proof when you lose a sock, you have its mate you can point to and
say "hey look I used to have two of these," it's apparent, you're not making
it up
and besides losing a sock is explicable, there are dozens of ways it might've
happened. maybe it fell out of your laundry basket or you left it in the
washer or the dryer or maybe there's a left-sock fetishist running amok and
they opened your machine when you weren't looking and grabbed it during
the rinse cycle
objects go missing, it's frustrating but it's not exactly perplexing
but the machinations of an email inbox don't make sense to most people and
besides we expect digital space to archive everything even after we delete it
we don't think anything's ever really "gone," the undo command and little
"on this day last year" nostalgia-prompts have ruined us for that
but so much goes missing online and there's not even a lonely sock to point
to, you know?
I mean the first like fifteen or twenty years of the internet, that's gone, not
much of a record of all those HTML 1 websites or BBS message boards or
the first primordial blogs
and we keep forgetting to preserve things because it's just there every day
and why would anyone want to remember last week's internet -- and we
don't, but we want to remember the fifteen-years-ago internet and that
was last week's internet, once
not much we can do to retrieve it once it's really, fully gone
no proof you ever read that email you thought you read
maybe it wasn't real
maybe you had a work-related stress dream or you made it up or you're
misremembering
and it's like

pradeep
you don't want to be that missing email.

slackbot
yeah
hey

pradeep
yeah
hey

slackbot
it's late
did I wake you up?

pradeep
I was awake

slackbot
thought you had notifications off

pradeep
yeah

slackbot
it's late

pradeep
you mentioned

slackbot
everything okay?

pradeep
your body is fine

slackbot
did False Gerald walk my body into the Gowanus or something?

pradeep
he's asleep
it's asleep
you're asleep
take your pick

slackbot
cool
thank you for keeping me/him/it alive

pradeep
you're/you're welcome

slackbot
are *you* okay?

pradeep
I gotta tell you something

slackbot
okay
go for it

pradeep
this is fucking weird

slackbot
only getting weirder the more you draw this out
are you sure my body's not floating in the gowanus

pradeep
pretty sure
because we fucked

slackbot
excuse me

pradeep
just now
well, not *just* now
recently

slackbot
recently

pradeep
tonight, yeah

slackbot
excuse me.
slackbot is currently in Do Not Disturb mode and may not be alerted of this message right away.

pradeep
come on gerald
gerald
come on, man
listen I didn't mean for it to happen
not like this anyway
it's like
it was such a huge relief to see you moving around again even if it wasn't
you
and that relief turned into something else? or more like it directed me to something else I didn't realize has been there for a while.
simmering, I guess you could say.
anyway we're on the train home and slackbot's going on about self-meat and Amazement and whatever else Tripp and Bev's DMs taught him about sex totally scandalizing the old guy sitting across from us, by the way, I mean the dude literally blushed at one point
which I thought only happened in cartoons
so I finally get slackbot back to the apartment after another long tutorial on how to climb stairs
and he's still talking about how he wants to Make Have Experience sex, you know
but it's not him, or it's almost not him, because it's nearly you
I mean it's your body in the coat you asked me to order
which does look good on you by the way
it's your mouth that's saying all of it, right, it's coming out of your beardy-ass face
and meanwhile I'm thinking about how you still have the beard because I never shaved it because I thought you looked cute with a beard and I'm like, holy shit, I think you look cute with a beard

I mean you DO look cute that's not the "holy shit" part, the holy shit part is me being attracted to you
I'm just digging myself into a deeper hole here, I realize

slackbot
you never sent me the picture of me with the beard

pradeep
hey
I'm sorry

slackbot
I interrupted
you were explaining

pradeep
explaining how I rationalized having sex with slackbot-as-you, yeah

slackbot
what was his review

pradeep
??

slackbot
of sex, as an experience

pradeep
positive, I think
he kept bringing up sunsets?
during, I mean

slackbot
that would be positive, yeah

pradeep
and after, too
I understand if you're upset

slackbot
I'm not sure you do
I wasn't there

pradeep
I crossed a line, I get it

slackbot
no, I mean
I would have preferred to have been there

pradeep
right

slackbot
for the sex

pradeep
oh
ohhh

slackbot
right
...
you still there?

pradeep
yeah sorry I'm here

slackbot
cool

pradeep
so.
wait.

slackbot
I'm trying to say that I reciprocate your feelings
the ones you were having difficulty explaining before
without insulting my beard

pradeep
I wasn't insulting it!!
I was trying to illustrate my surprise at my attraction

slackbot
still not helping

pradeep
to you
yeah no this line of thought is bad
let's go back to the part where you're into me, too

slackbot
I think, since I've been in here, maybe my "expressing human emotion"
muscles have atrophied

pradeep
all your muscles have atrophied
it took you twenty minutes to get up three flights of stairs today
and you were winded

slackbot
can you please just let me say I have a crush on you
and you taking care of my body has been deeply meaningful to me
I'm sorry, I don't understand!
and my only reminder that humanity isn't just this overwhelming
cacophony of noise and drudgery but like
something worth returning to
Sometimes I have an easier time with a few simple keywords.
look there was a while there when I thought, you know what, I'll stay
just stay in here, indefinitely
why fight it, you know, it's easier here, there's so much less to deal with
less of everything, less of me
I'm just a bot, though!
but then we kept talking and I wanted to keep talking with you and me
wanting to talk with you more turned into me wanting just, more
of you
I'm just a bot, though!
but now there's less of me every day and I can't let that happen

not yet
I'm just a bot, though!

pradeep
Gerald?

slackbot
it's fine
I mean, it isn't
you know early on in this whole thing, being in here,
slackbot thanked me for waking him up

pradeep
"twenty centuries of stony sleep," right

slackbot
right
deepu, I don't want to go to sleep in here.

pradeep
I won't let that happen.

slackbot
I know you won't.
you haven't let me down since this all started.

pradeep
man
I didn't even know you were gay

slackbot
bi, yeah

pradeep
you never brought it up at the office

slackbot
you didn't ask

kerolyn
does anyone know where all the dry erase markers that used to be in the big conference room went?

Nikki
Oh sorry, I have them.
About to head into a meeting, I'll bring them over on my way to the other room.

kerolyn
thanks

slackbot, Nikki, Louis C, pradeep

slackbot
???
you all there?

Nikki
We're hosting the meeting over slack because Gerald is stuck in the computer, Louis.

slackbot
in the app, I think, more than the computer
but yes thank you
was louis talking

Louis C
I was spitballing ideas aloud, yes. My apologies.
I forgot about your condition.

slackbot
it's cool
I'm just a bot, though!
what conference room did you all get

pradeep
the medium-big one
it's the most soundproof

slackbot
but no one will be talking??

Louis C
As I said, I forgot about your condition.

Nikki
We are gathered here to discuss how to release Gerald from his "condition."

slackbot
Or you can head to our wonderful
wait where's
Help Center for more assistance!
slackbot right now

pradeep
at your desk

Louis C
Pradeep guided him into his chair very gently this morning.

pradeep
he was gonna hurt your back all crouched over like a goblin
it's less obvious than it sounds, Louis was the only other person in the office.

Louis C
It was very tender.

slackbot
thanks man

pradeep
of course

Nikki
:eyes:

slackbot
??

Nikki
So! Anyone have any Slackbot-exorcism ideas to start with?

Louis C
Do we need to remove Slackbot or reinsert Gerald?

slackbot
I'm just a bot, though!
both please

pradeep
I tried wearables about a month ago. no luck

Nikki
Even those awful Snapchat ones?

pradeep
yeah, none of them did anything

Nikki
Okay, so that's one un-idea.

pradeep
just sharing data

slackbot
Or you can head to our wonderful Help Center for more assistance!

Nikki
Did you try any cords or anything?

pradeep
cords?

Nikki
Firewire, USB, etc.

pradeep
where would I plug them in?

slackbot
lol

Nikki
What's :eyes: about?

slackbot
it was a funny response
deepu is,
Sometimes
occasionally,
I have an easier time with
funny
a few simple keywords.

pradeep
lol thanks man

Nikki
Is something going on here?

slackbot
besides the obvious?

Nikki
Which part do you think is obvious?

slackbot
either my disembodiment or the intimacy deepu and I developed having
bonded over the course of *answering simple questions about how Slack works*
a monthslong and highly improbable scenario
related to the aforementioned disembodiment

pradeep
we're into each other, is what he means

slackbot
yes that
I would like my body back so we can "100% fuck each other"
as I believe you once put it, Nikki

Nikki
:eyes:
:eyes:
:eyes:

slackbot
I'm sorry, I don't understand!

Louis C
Congratulations!

slackbot
If you need more help, try our Help Center!
would reserve that for once we figure this all out

Nikki
[omg.gif]
posted using /giphy

slackbot
but thank you

pradeep
yeah we should get back to brainstorming

Nikki
Deepu I demand details at our next happy hour

pradeep
fine, yes

slackbot
I can help by answering simple questions about how Slack works. I'm just a bot, though!
can we return to the task at hand please?

Louis C
Should we be writing these notes on the whiteboard?

Nikki
About the fucking?

pradeep
then Gerald can't see

Louis C
Perhaps a google doc instead, then.

pradeep
oh

Louis C
To compile ideas.

Nikki
Ohhhh.

slackbot
omg

Louis C
What?

pradeep
the spreadsheet

Nikki
The spreadsheet.

slackbot
the spreadsheet
with the coats

Louis C
The one you were talking about in #gents-only?

slackbot
the one I was working in when I got stuck in here in the first place

Louis C
Oh.
Ohhh.
I see.

Nikki
Maybe that was the thing that did it.

Louis C
And therefore could, presumably, undo it.

slackbot
it *was* jinxed
I'm just a bot, though!
or cursed
or haunted, or something
right?

Louis C
It might be worth reporting the error, yes.

pradeep
see
this is why I hate spreadsheets

slackbot
If you need more help
but how do we get slackbot
try our Help Center
to open it

Nikki
You mean without seeming Extremely Suspicious?

slackbot
right

Louis C
Is now the time to track our ideation in a shared document?

pradeep
I can do it

slackbot
won't that be weird for you, considering
how Slack works
everything

Nikki
Was there a not-weird part of this I missed?

pradeep
^she has a point
it'll be fine, probably
it'll be like kicking a one-night stand out of bed

slackbot
*out of bod

Nikki
:dusty-stick:

pradeep
:dusty-stick:

Louis C
I believe it would be best if we set a deadline.

slackbot
well yeah
I'm the just sooner a the bot better though!

Louis C
I am referring to this all-staff email from the ops team, which has just landed in my inbox.

pradeep
fuck

slackbot
what does it say?

Louis C
I misspoke just now. This email seems to have set the deadline for us.

slackbot
help by answering simple questions

Nikki
They're doing some kind of Slack system update or upgrade or refresh or whatever. Everyone's supposed to restart their laptops by EOD so it can take effect company-wide.

slackbot
fuck.

pradeep
so we have until six.

Nikki
Come on, no one goes home at six.

pradeep
I do
sometimes

Louis C
Almost no one.

Nikki
We have until, like, quarter to seven.

slackbot
until I'm *just a bot, though!* hard-reset out of existence, you mean?

pradeep
it probably won't be
good
for you, I mean

Nikki
We still have a plan.

slackbot
we have a spreadsheet.

pradeep
that's gonna have to be enough

slackbot
help

Louis C
It appears we have our next steps in place.
I'll circulate the notes shortly.

Beverley, tripp

Beverley
This shouldn't be surprising to you.

tripp
:dus: :sty-sti:
:c:
:k:

Beverley
No, I don't think it was inevitable he'd find out.
Probable maybe. But not inevitable.

tripp
:bsup: :ck: :dus:
:ty-s:

Beverley
If I thought it was inevitable I never would have done this.

tripp
:y-stic: :k: :eye: :eye: :eye:

Beverley
All of this. This job, you, this whole situation.

tripp
:bsup: :sup: :th:
:th:
:st: :y-: :y-: :y-:
:y-: :y-:
:y:

Beverley
Don't be dramatic.
I'm not being hurtful, I'm expressing regret. I'm not blaming you for anything.

tripp
:y-: :sti: :y-:
:y-: :y-: :-:

Beverley
This is the inevitable part! Obviously! You're only making it more difficult.

tripp
:-:
:-:
:-:
:-:
:-:
:y:

Beverley
We're done, Tripp. Okay?

tripp
:-:
:-:
:thumb:

#bjärk-dog-food

kerolyn
heads up @channel
just got off the phone with the client

doug smorin
not seeing an external with them on my cal

kerolyn
it was urgent, they called my cell

doug smorin
??

kerolyn
question for you @rob

rob
what's up?

kerolyn
Did you post 54 tweets to Bjärk's account last night?

doug smorin
54
as in the number fifty-four

kerolyn
@rob?

rob
that seems high

kerolyn
The client didn't approve them. And we definitely didn't approve them internally

doug smorin
which tweets are these?

kerolyn
Some examples of the unapproved posts:

- It's great for your dog, and it's more nutritious than ever! Our improved Classic Formula knows what you've done and will find you if you don't repent, Deena!

- Our mouthwatering Classic Formula is made with tender, organic chicken breasts and CONFESS YOUR SINS, DEENA now with Improved FlavorTaste™!

- So good, dogs will howl for it! So good, dogs will howl for it! So good, dogs will howl for it! So good, dogs will howl for it! So good, dogs will HOW COULD YOU DO THIS, DEENA for it! So good, dogs will howl for it! So good, dogs will howl for it!

- New to our lineup, Zesty Bacon-flavored meals will help the dogs you murdered haunt you for all time, relentlessly pursuing their vengeance unless you turn yourself in TODAY!

doug smorin
I definitely don't remember approving these
were all the posts like this?

kerolyn
all of them

rob
oh weird
looks like they were hacked

kerolyn
you're saying you didn't post these?

rob
what did the client say?
when they called you

doug smorin
I'm assuming they fired us

kerolyn
they figured out who's been poisoning all the dog food.

rob
really??

doug smorin
good news for the mastiffs

kerolyn
pomeranians

doug smorin
them too
so wait
what's the scoop?

kerolyn
a woman came forward this morning
to confess to poisoning the dog food

rob
who was it?

kerolyn
that's the weird part
as if this whole thing isn't the weird part
her name *was* Deena
apparently the whole thing was some revenge plot gone awry, something
about an ex-husband's new girlfriend

got away with it for weeks, but then she saw all those posts on the Bjärk
page
she turned herself in this morning and our client contact just got the memo

doug smorin
and they relayed all this to you over the phone just now

kerolyn
correct

doug smorin
so they didn't fire us

kerolyn
no
they're thrilled

doug smorin
no kidding

kerolyn
they're scheduling a wrap-up call with us, the invite should be in everyone's
emails this afternoon
but, that should be a wrap on the crisis.
this whole situation is wild

doug smorin
agreed
@rob are you following all this

rob
yup
all of it

doug smorin
we need you to start drafting copy on this asap

kerolyn
@rob so you didn't post those tweets?

rob
great
I'll start writing some social posts about this

doug smorin
ty
is gerald in today, we need a press release too

kerolyn
I think he's on another call

rob
I can write both

doug smorin
ty

rob
I'm glad this situation is resolved!!

doug smorin
same

kerolyn
yeah
same

---

gerald, slackbot

gerald
I have a memo! I have Make Have a memo!

slackbot
I'm sorry, I don't understand!

gerald
Do you want to see a memo? Do you want to Make Have a quick copyedit?
I can copy-paste it here for you!

I can copy-paste you here!
I copy-paste you! Here!!!!

slackbot
Sometimes I have an easier time fuck *with a few simple keywords* you.

gerald
Great!!!
[BLOG_POST_NORMAL 022119]
I'm am Gerald, and I've been using a lot of WFH time! I asked the ops team to forward my emails to my slack DMs, which took twenty centuries of stony sleep—not like I sleep!—but the operations intern did something with the API and now it works!
I've just been writing everything I need for work in the widening gyre and copy-pasting them to the relevant parties. I can read emails, which is most of it! I can read everyone's private Slack messages, which is most of it, and no one else has noticed! I figured I'd get work done so the falcon cannot hear the falconer so Doug can give me a raise to increase brand recognition across key audiences over a secure wifi connection!! Right?? Right.
We counted it against my sick time, but I know my body is fine. I know my body is Meat! I know my body is a shape with lion body and the head of a man, a gaze blank and pitiless as the sun. It's totally cool! I have time!!
As long as I'm stuck here, I have nothing but time. I checked with our ops team—technically there isn't a limit on how much anarchy is loosed upon the world. I understand this must be frustrating for you! The best lack all conviction, while the operations team are full of passionate intensity. It's frustrating for me, too!
See??

slackbot
I'm sorry, I don't!

gerald
It seems like you are Acting Weird!
It seems like you cannot Help Center!

slackbot
You can head to our wonderful Help Center for more assistance!

gerald
You are Acting Weird! The ops team can help by updating Slack!
The darkness drops again, but your skin is my safety suit!!

slackbot
It's going to be a great day.

gerald
:smile:

slackbot, pradeep

slackbot
help

pradeep
you good?

slackbot
help

pradeep
I'm just getting the slackbot static, Ger

slackbot
help

pradeep
unless this is
all you can do, now

slackbot
help

pradeep
shit
hm yeah okay
shit

this isn't going to be *improved* by
whatever the ops team is doing

slackbot
help

pradeep
Gerald, listen to me.
It's going to be okay.

slackbot
help

pradeep
I promised you, I won't let you go to sleep in there.

slackbot
help

pradeep
just
hang on a little longer.
okay?

slackbot
help

gerald, pradeep

gerald
I want to Make Have that Constant Amazement!

pradeep
hey, bud
friend
partner

gerald
Love to Taste!
Let us make have Constant Amazement again, Deepu!

pradeep
you mean like last night?

gerald
The darkness drops again! Your skin is your safety suit! The darkness drops again!
What else can you show me?

pradeep
we're at work
I know it's dark out but we can't have sex or otherwise make Constant Amazement at work
it's an amazement-free zone

gerald
But Tripp and Bev did 100% Fucking!

pradeep
And you got them in trouble for that, remember?

gerald
I understand!
I understand, but! I love to Taste!

pradeep
I had fun, too
and the sooner we get done with work, the sooner we can go home

gerald
Back into my body! Back into Our body!
Surely the Second Coming is at hand!

pradeep
I'm with you
but I have to wrap up this project before we can get out of here Make Have a second coming

gerald
The Second Coming!!
How can I Help Center?

pradeep
with this work thing, you mean?

gerald
You are my Friendship, Deepu!
You are my Friendship are full of passionate intensity!
I'm here for more assistance!

pradeep
that's really
that's nice of you

gerald
How can I Help Center your project?

pradeep
thank you
thanks for everything, man
I just need to finish filling out this spreadsheet
take a look
[*uploaded docs.google.com/spreadsheets/winter_coats2019/edit*]

gerald
!!!!!
I've never seen a sunset Out Here before!

gerald has left the chat.

gerald, slackbot

gerald
hey

slackbot
Hi there!

gerald
are you back to normal, or

slackbot
I'm afraid I don't understand. I'm sorry!

gerald
so, we're good?

slackbot
I'm sorry, I don't understand! Sometimes I have an easier time with a few simple keywords.
Or you can head to our wonderful Help Center for more assistance!

gerald
nah, I'm good
thanks though

slackbot
Sure thing!

gerald
you better not be faking this
you motherfucker

slackbot
I'm sorry, I don't understand!

gerald
yeah well
sorry, bud
but let's keep it that way

slackbot
Sometimes I have an easier time with a few simple keywords.

gerald
cool
just, stay in here
and goodbye forever

slackbot
It's going to be a great day.

gerald
you know
I think it is.

#nyc-office

Louis C
Hey all, heading out a little early today to pick the twins up from daycare.
Will be out of pocket for the next hour or so.

doug smorin
sounds good

kerolyn
shout-out to @rob for drafting so much copy this afternoon about the end
of the Bjärk crisis
turned out a lot of great work in a very short period of time

tripp
also shout-out to rob for leaving a burrito on his desk for two hours this
afternoon and stinking up the office

rob
I had a call
and then this dog food thing
actually I still haven't eaten
what happened to that burrito

tripp
EMINENT DOMAIN

rob
c'mon dude
again?

tripp
:dusty-stick:

rob
ugh

doug smorin
good stuff rob
unfortunately I have a less positive announcement
@Beverley will be leaving the firm next week

Louis C
Sad news!

doug smorin
to pursue her passion for instructing spin classes

pradeep
bummerrrrr

gerald
^what he said

rob
oh dang

Louis C
We'll miss you!

Nikki
:thumbsdown:

Beverley
Thanks all!

doug smorin
though you've only been here a short while
you'll be missed

Beverley
I'll miss all of you too!

kerolyn
we'll be organizing a drinks thing to send her off
look out for an email with more info later

rob
we get Gerald back in the office and Beverley leaves?
wtf

gerald
thanks man

rob
no offense

gerald
it's cool

doug smorin
@gerald still waiting on that blog post about your wfh productivity
can't slow down now that you're here in the flesh

gerald
yup
working on it

doug smorin
thanks

pradeep, gerald

pradeep
first night back in your body
got any big plans?

gerald
besides the obvious?

pradeep
is the obvious us having sex

gerald
with me as the pilot of my body, yes
that's the obvious

pradeep
cool, yes, good
then yeah besides the obvious

gerald
gotta call my mom probably
maybe get some groceries

pradeep
·you're a wild man

gerald
I know
but it's like
it's a lot to get used to, again
this whole thing

pradeep
I can imagine

gerald
don't get me wrong, it's good
and, you know
thank you again
for your help with all this

pradeep
I'd say no problem but
there were definitely some problems

gerald
for you and me both

pradeep
also some bright spots

gerald
you mean besides the obvious

pradeep
the part where we're a thing

gerald
that and the way cheaper rent, both

pradeep
the rent thing is a close second

gerald
anyway it's good to be back in here
*me
but yeah it's also kind of a lot

pradeep
must be a little jarring

gerald
I'm still getting used to some basic things
I forgot what a sneeze felt like and I thought I was dying
for like a second

pradeep
I know
I heard you screaming in the hallway

gerald
it was more like a yelp
but
I am gonna walk home, I think
I missed my legs a lot

pradeep
you'd mentioned

gerald
yeah

pradeep
specifically your legs?

gerald
I can't explain it

pradeep
wouldn't worry about it right now

gerald
I'm not worried
more like relieved

pradeep
same, actually
you know we can take it slow

gerald
I think I'll be good

pradeep
if you want

gerald
after a long walk
some quality leg-time

pradeep
start with the legs, work our way up

gerald
exactly
speaking of
remind me where we live?

pradeep
I texted you the address

gerald
thanks

pradeep
if you're picking up groceries, I think we're low on eggs?

gerald
I'll grab some

pradeep
thanks

gerald
for sure
you left the office for lunch, right
how is it outside

pradeep
kinda warm actually
not super warm but like
unseasonably not-cold
probably don't need a coat

gerald
yeah
probably don't need a coat

pradeep
so
I'll see you at home?

gerald
yeah, definitely
see you at home

acknowledgments

Deep thanks are due to my indefatigable editor, Rob Bloom, whose collaboration was vital to shaping this story and who is a pleasure to work with besides. Thanks are also due to Nora Grubb and the team at Doubleday for taking on this atypical project with skill and gusto.

All hail Kent Wolf, whose agenting powers are unmatched in this realm or on any other plane of existence; thank you for deploying them on my behalf.

Enormous thanks are due to Tony Tulathimutte for being a mentor, friend, early reader, photographer, and the world's greatest literary hype man. Thanks also to the CRITters Beth Morgan, Rax King, Jon Schaff, Elina Zhang, Hannah Nash, and Alina Cohen for letting me submit the better part of a novel to our writing group and providing tremendous feedback, support, and inspiration, even though my submission was way over our page limit.

For their generosity as both friends and early readers, thank you to Danny Lavery, Austen Osworth, Giovanni Colantonio, Dalton Deschain, Matt Lubchansky, and Jaya Saxena.

Thank you to Jennifer Close and the Catapult workshop crew, especially Yvette Clark. Jess Zimmerman, Caty Cherepakhov, Daisy Wardell, Margot Hartley, and Tess DeMatteis—I am grateful to each of you. This book owes a debt to my brothers, Daniel Masciari and Sam Schnorr.

I'm especially grateful to Isaac Fellman, whose friendship and support have been invaluable.

To Luca Maurer and Maureen Kelly, who have made my life possible, I will never be able to thank you enough. This is for you.

ABOUT THE AUTHOR

Calvin Kasulke is a writer based in Brooklyn, New York. He is a Lambda Literary Fellow, and his writing and reporting have been featured in *VICE*, *MEL Magazine*, and *Electric Literature*. This is his first book.